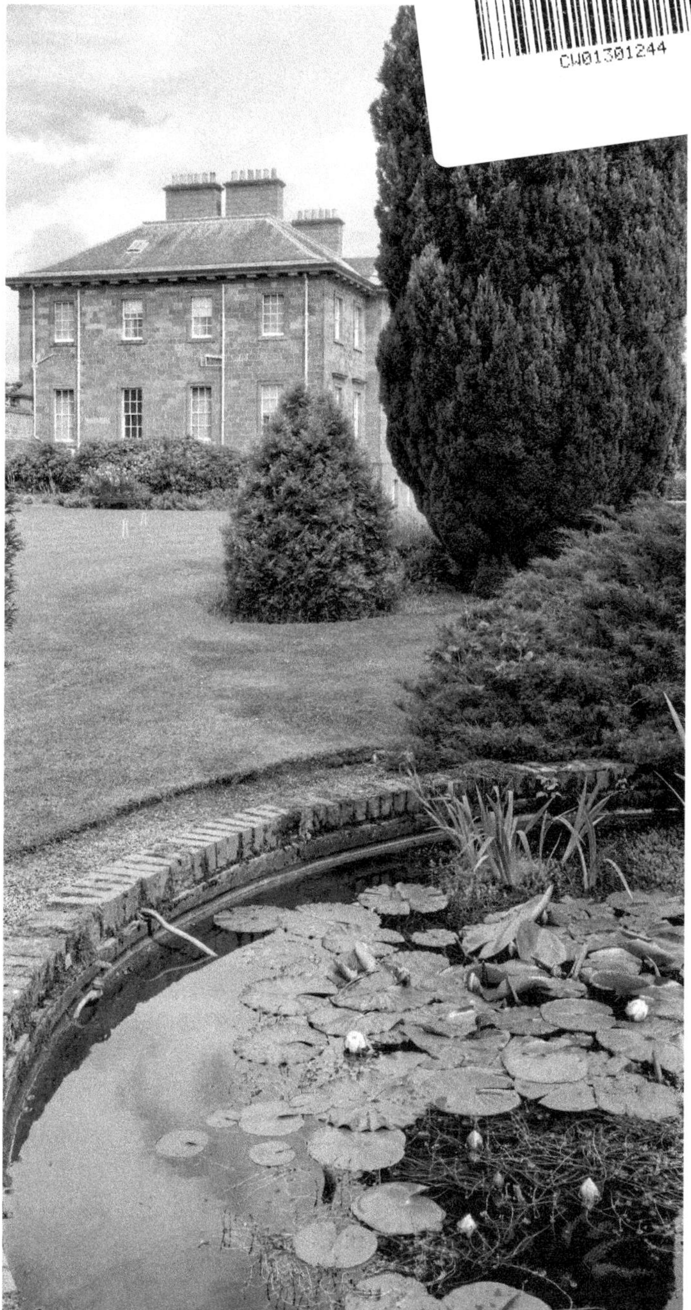

NEVER BEGUILE A BODYGUARD
Guarding Her Heart Series, Book 1

Published by Edwards and Williams
Copyright © 2023 by Regina Lundgren

All rights reserved. Except for use in any review, the reproduction or utilization of this work in whole or in part in any form by any electronic, mechanical or other means, now known or hereinafter invented, including xerography, photocopying and recording, or in any information storage or retrieval system, is forbidden without the written permission of the publisher.

This is a work of fiction. Names, characters, places and incidents are either the product of the author's imagination or are used fictitiously, and any resemblance to actual persons, living or dead, business establishments, events or locales is entirely coincidental.

Printed in the USA.

Cover Design and Interior Format
© THE KILLION GROUP, INC.

BOOK
ONE
GUARDING HER HEART

Never Beguile a Bodyguard

REGINA SCOTT

To all members of the Air Force, Army, Navy, Marines, and Coast Guard, who protect us, and to the Lord, who provides, always.

CHAPTER ONE

London, England
September 1825

WHEN ALL ELSE failed, a lady had only her composure to rely upon.

Abigail Winchester believed that, but all else had failed, and she felt far from composed as she clutched the edge of the hack's worn leather seat. The hired carriage had come to a stop before a tall, elegant townhouse in a fashionable square. Nothing about that green-lacquered door hinted of danger. But she knew why she expected it to come leaping out.

She glanced up and down the street. A footman swept the stairs at number eleven. A governess exited number nine with her two charges for an outing.

A governess like she had been until a week ago.

"You getting out, miss?" the hack driver called from the bench. "This was where you paid to go."

It was. A week in a ladies' lodging house in a far less fashionable part of town had put a considerable dent in her meager funds, and she could not shake the feeling that she was being followed. She needed help, and the list of people who might be willing to extend that help was pitiably small. Everyone had distanced themselves from her—family, friends, acquaintances—since the full extent of her father's scandal had become clear. Even Preston had defected, and she'd thought to be married to him by now.

And so, here she was. Staring at the door of a house belonging to a lady to whom she could scarcely claim acquaintance. Her only hope for help, unless she was willing to approach *him*.

Yes, to her shame, she had considered that. Finn Huber of the Batavarian Imperial Guard had shown her considerable kindness when she had been tending to the children at a house party given by the Duchess of Wey. He had been guarding the crown prince and his brother, who had been attending the party with their betrotheds, the duke's two oldest daughters. But he had made time to come visit the children, who had positively doted on him. So had she, truth be told. And she could not ascribe the feeling entirely to the glitter of gold braid crossing that broad chest.

But there she had even less claim to acquaintance. And the papers she studied so assiduously for news of the scandal had reported that the Batavarian delegation had departed England, homebound at last. She liked thinking of him among the mountains he had so eloquently extolled.

"Miss?" The hack driver's voice had become more insistent. "If you're going to loiter, I'll have to charge you."

Enough dithering. She had survived her parents' deaths and the scandal by keeping her head high, her smile pleasant, and her feet moving. She slid the top bolt, pushed open the door, gathered her blue poplin skirts, and climbed down onto the pavement.

"Forgive me for delaying you," she said to the driver. "I merely had to screw my courage to the sticking place."

He must never have read Shakespeare, or seen *MacBeth* at the theatre, for he frowned at her. "Good day, then." He clucked to his horses and drove off.

Abigail focused on the door again, which seemed unaccountably far from the edge of the street. She had faced down demanding creditors, newspaper reporters seeking secrets, and curious children in a schoolroom. What was this to all that?

She marched to the door, climbed the few steps, seized the brass knocker—which was shaped like the head of a snarling lion—and rapped at the panel.

An elderly butler with a ring of wispy white hair opened the door. He was tall enough that he could look down at her with his rheumy blue eyes, or perhaps it was only the way his long nose pointed in her direction, as if accusing her of some crime.

Composure, Abigail.

"Miss Winchester to see Lady Belfort," she said, pleased that her voice came out confident and cordial.

"Her ladyship is currently engaged," he wheezed. "But if you will wait in the entry, I will determine whether she will admit you as well."

It was the time of day for calls. She should have thought of that. Once she would have had a withdrawing room full of ladies and gentlemen to entertain or would have been out calling herself, her mother at her side.

What a charming bonnet, Miss Winchester. The flowers suit your sunny temperament.

May I importune your hand for a dance at the ball on Tuesday evening, Miss Winchester? I vow you are light as eiderdown on your feet.

Why would your father agree to fund a charlatan, Miss Winchester? Did you aid him in making such a disastrous decision?

"Delighted," she said, stepping over the threshold. The butler turned to start up the stairs.

She tilted her head to follow his path, but the movement was echoed beside her, and she turned to meet her own gaze in the mirror next to the door. The young lady looking back at her had warm blond hair tucked up inside a straw bonnet lined with satin that matched the blue of her eyes. She looked entirely comfortable in the luxurious surroundings.

She seemed to have developed a knack for dissembling.

Below the mirror stood a mahogany bench. Did her ladyship have so many petitioners who must wait for a moment of her time? At the very thought, her legs folded to deposit her on the seat as if having done their duty by getting her here.

But something else was moving on the stair, a streak of grey that resolved itself into a cat. It dropped onto the marble-tiled floor and padded closer. A lovely creature, with a plumed tail and white wound round its throat and down its belly like a gentleman's cravat, the cat stopped directly in front of her and regarded her with eyes the color of copper pennies.

Abigail smiled. "Good morning. And how are you faring today?"

The cat cocked its head. Was it wondering why she spoke to it? Surely others had been tempted to pour their troubles into those alert ears.

The cat straightened, stalked closer, then hopped up into her lap.

"Well, aren't you a darling?" Abigail said. "Thank you for making me feel welcome."

The cat turned twice, then settled on her skirts as if preparing for a long nap.

The fears clinging to her burned away like mist in the sunlight. She ran a hand gently down the fur. A purr rumbled against her thigh. Why were her eyes stinging? She'd known kindness before. It simply seemed so long ago.

A noise above had her peering upward once more. The butler was making his stately way down the stairs. He did not appear concerned to find the pet of the house curled up in her lap. Indeed, she thought she caught a hint of a smile on those thin lips.

"That is very good," he said with a nod, as if she had passed some sort of test. "Her ladyship will be delighted."

Interesting how he stressed his employer's title. Was he trying to impress upon her the unsuitability of her claiming acquaintance? Or was he so very pleased about the lady's elevation to the peerage? Lord and Lady Belfort had been awarded their titles only recently, as the papers liked to remind their readers, and by the King of Batavaria, for services to the crown. His lordship was a savvy solicitor with connections in high places.

"Then she will see me?" Abigail asked.

"She will see you," he promised. "And she has sent an escort."

Abigail glanced down at the cat in her lap. "So I see."

"Not that escort."

Her head jerked up at the voice from the stairs, and for a moment, she was certain she had conjured him from thin air. Finn Huber, dressed today like a London gentleman in a navy coat and fawn trousers instead of the black and gold of his uniform, was descending toward her, dark hair combed back from his face, smile warm, and amber eyes alight.

Hope leaped up, then crashed.

How was she to explain her deplorable situation to Lady Belfort in front of the one person whose admiration she most craved?

———

Finn's heart seemed to be pounding louder than the drum calling the march. He had expected to feel elation knowing he was moving into a new future in England, but instead, his thoughts had persisted on dwelling on what he was leaving behind.

On who he was leaving behind.

And now she was here, against all odds. He couldn't seem to stop his smile.

He came to a halt at the bottom of the stairs and clapped his fist to his chest in salute. "Miss Winchester."

"Mr. Huber." She started to rise, then seemed to recall the cat on her lap. Lady Belfort's pet reached out her paws in a leisurely stretch, and cast him a glance as if chiding him for depriving her of such a pleasant place to nap.

"Forgive me, Fortune," he said with a bow. "But I have need of the lady."

The cat deigned to drop to the ground and stalked off toward the stairs.

"You speak to her too?" Miss Winchester asked, rising at last.

A distinguished member of the Batavarian Imperial Guard, who had fought in the war with Napoleon, should not blush, yet heat burned his cheeks. "You will come to understand that Fortune holds a special place in this house."

Mr. Cowls, the butler, snorted, then turned the noise into a genteel cough. "You may tell her ladyship that Fortune approved of Miss Winchester."

He would never have doubted that. Since coming to know Lady Belfort and her circle, he had been regaled by any number of stories about the cat. Fortune was said to have matched the Duke and Duchess of Wey, the Earl and Countess of Carrolton, the Marquess and Marchioness of Kendall, and Sir Matthew and Lady Bateman. He had seen for himself how the cat had helped orchestrate the match linking his prince to Lady Larissa, and Count Montalban, the prince's brother, to Lady Calantha, both daughters of the Duke of Wey. It was said that if Fortune approved of you, your character must be very fine indeed.

He was honored to have earned that approval himself.

Small wonder the woman before him had earned it.

From the first time he had met her, in the schoolroom at the duke's estate, he had appreciated her gentle smile, her kind way of guiding the children under her care. And who would not admire hair as rich as honey and eyes as blue as the sky over the Batavarian mountains?

He held out his arm. "May I escort you to Lady Belfort?"

"As it appears to be a little distance, I think I shall contrive." Her smile took the sting from the words, and Finn contented himself with walking beside her up the stairs.

"We have been seeking you," he told her.

She started, but her voice remained pleasant. "Seeking me? Whatever for?"

"Sir Matthew and Lady Bateman require a new governess," he explained. "But when they approached the employment agency that placed you, they were told you had disappeared from your last position, and no one knew where to find you."

He would not admit that the thought of her alone and friendless in the great metropolis had made sleep difficult since he'd heard she'd disappeared. He had felt helpless twice in his life. He did not intend to put himself in a position to feel that clammy sickness again.

She did not answer, but then, they had reached the landing and the withdrawing room that opened off it. She stopped in the doorway, as if unable to go on.

Tanner, Keller, and Roth, his comrades who had also decided to remain in England when the prince had sailed for home, stood at the sight of her and clapped fist to chest. Her gaze darted from them to the lady seated on the sofa.

"You remember Mr. Keller and Mr. Roth from the house party," Finn encouraged her. "Mr. Tanner is also a member of the Imperial Guard."

"Former member," Tanner said with a smile. "And it

is a pleasure to meet you at last, Miss Winchester. I have heard nothing but praise for your skill." He nudged Keller beside him. "Though I would have thought someone would have mentioned your beauty."

Keller, the youngest of them, blushed. He could get away with it with those guileless blue eyes and round cheeks. Many had underestimated him, to their sorrow.

Roth, the eldest, sent Tanner a dark look and crossed his arms over his chest. With raven hair and eyes like the steel of his sword, he still looked like what he was, a battle-hardened fighter of an elite band of warriors, who suddenly found themselves in need of a different future.

"Yes, welcome, Miss Winchester," Lady Belfort said. She also looked her part: a grand lady, with dark hair piled up in complicated braids at the back of her head and tailored skirts the same shade of lavender as her eyes. Her smile broadened. "And here is the final member of our party."

Fortune wound past them, somehow managing to brush both Miss Winchester's skirts and Finn's boots before making her way to her mistress' side.

"Mr. Cowls asked me to inform you that Fortune approved of Miss Winchester," Finn told her.

"Well, of course she would," Roth said with a shake of his head.

Lady Belfort waited for her pet to jump up onto her lap before resting a hand on the fur. "That is very good news indeed. I have come to rely on Fortune's insights, as my own are sometimes colored by wishes instead of reality. Please, Miss Winchester, be welcome. The gentlemen were just leaving."

"Dismissed," Roth agreed, with a nod to nudge them all toward the door. "We will be here at first light, as requested, your ladyship."

"I'm fairly sure I said half past eight," she corrected him

as he started toward the door, Keller and Tanner in front. "But you will be welcome, regardless."

Keller shot Finn a grin as he passed. Tanner tipped his head toward Miss Winchester and widened his eyes as if impressed. Roth sent him a look as sharp as a cutlass.

He was expected to fall in line. Something in him protested. But he would not question his duty. It had kept him sane for too many years. He turned to follow them.

"A moment, Mr. Huber," Lady Belfort called. "I may require your advice."

He hesitated. So did Roth.

"She is our patroness," Roth hissed. "Do what she asks of you. We will await you in the park across the street."

Finn nodded, and his leader continued down the stairs.

Finn ventured into the room and took the chair Roth had vacated, next to the sofa and across from Miss Winchester, where he could see both ladies and the exits easily. Habit. A bodyguard to the king must always be on the alert for danger.

"Now, then," Lady Belfort said, leaning back on the sofa as if she had no such concerns. "How might I be of assistance, Miss Winchester?"

She glanced between them, then must have come to a decision, for she raised her chin. "I find myself in a difficult position, your ladyship. I have been fortunate in my employment thus far, but I was forced into resigning from my last post, and I believe I am being followed now. I was told that you help gentlewomen down on their luck. I would seem to qualify."

Finn's shoulders tightened with each word. "Who would trouble you like this?"

She kept her gaze on Lady Belfort. "I do not know who has been following me, but I can guess why. My father was involved in a scandal a few years ago. My previous employer apparently discovered the fact and made things unpleasant for me. Others seem to think I might have been involved. I can assure you, I had no knowledge of the scheme."

A father's decisions affected all those around him, he had cause to know. Some of his agitation must have been evident, for Fortune dropped to her feet to pad closer. He would not allow himself to come under the calming sway of those copper eyes. That anyone would wish Abigail Winchester harm was serious.

"Then I am very glad you came to me," Lady Belfort said. "I intend to find the four Imperial Guards positions here in England. They will be joining me tomorrow at my estate in Surrey, Rose Hill, in the guest cottage next to my home. As my husband is currently out of the country, traveling with the Batavarian delegation to Württemberg to ratify the agreement between the countries and England, I would benefit from having a lady companion, like you."

Miss Winchester's lower lip trembled. "How kind, your ladyship."

How kind indeed. And how fitting. With Lady Belford her patroness as well, he would not have to concern himself with Abigail Winchester's safety. He could move into the future with no fear of losing his heart again. It had never fully healed from the last time he had been assigned to guard a lady.

"A temporary position only, you understand," her ladyship continued, "but it would allow me to assess your skills and find you a more suitable position when it is finished. In the meantime, to ensure our safety, I will ask you to act as her bodyguard, Mr. Huber."

CHAPTER TWO

A BODYGUARD? ABIGAIL KNEW she was grinning and carefully schooled her face. But how could she not grin? Those who thought to punish her for her father's mistakes would certainly think twice at the sight of Finn Huber beside her. That lean, powerful body, those golden brown eyes, like a lion's in their ferocity. Even Preston Netherfield, who she had thought the epitome of gentlemanly valor, would have swallowed hard.

But was it fair to involve him in her troubles? Hadn't enough people been hurt?

"I would not wish to be a burden," she said to Lady Belfort.

Somehow, she thought her ladyship also subscribed to the view of composure being a lady's best defense. The only indication of amusement on her face was a slight arch of her dark brow.

"No burden," she said. "It is best to keep Mr. Huber busy while I find him a permanent position."

Lady Belfort hadn't asked his permission, merely given him an order. But he seemed to have mastered the art of composure as well, for he inclined his head, giving Abigail no insight into his thoughts on the matter.

"Can you be ready at half past eight tomorrow?" Lady Belfort pressed.

She wasn't sure what she'd expected when she'd approached the lady—perhaps a governess position in a remote corner of Cornwall? But she could not doubt this assignment would be better. Rose Hill was near the duke's holdings along the Thames, if she remembered correctly. The area had seemed thin of Society. Surely few there would have invested in the far off country of Poyais, and fewer still would know the connection of one Arthur Winchester, her father, in the scheme that was still unfolding in England, France, and the South American countries. And Mr. Huber for her own personal bodyguard?

A shiver went through her. It wasn't fear.

He was watching her with that stillness she admired. Like a boulder, unscathed by wind or rain, undaunted by ice or heat. A rock a lady could lean upon when her strength failed her.

Funny how all the rocks in her life—her father, Preston—had crumbled. Even Cornelius Benchley, her father's dearest friend, who she'd considered an uncle, had distanced himself from her, claiming she would be better off without another millstone around her neck. Did she dare take a chance on Finn Huber?

Composure. She was not offering him her life. She was accepting a temporary position that might secure her a better future.

She rose, then held out a hand to prevent him from doing likewise.

"Yes, your ladyship," she said. "Thank you for the opportunity, and thank you, Mr. Huber, for agreeing to look out for my welfare. Until tomorrow."

She dropped a curtsey, but he was at her side as she straightened.

"Since I am to be your bodyguard," he said, "I should see you home."

"Very wise," Lady Belfort said before Abigail could argue.

And truly, did she want to argue? How glorious to

know she need not look over her shoulder. She could feel her lungs expanding at the thought.

"Thank you, Mr. Huber," she said again, and he fell into step beside her.

When they reached the ground floor, he held up his hand. "Stay here. I will tell my colleagues to continue to the palace. I can call for a carriage to join them later."

She nodded.

He left, shutting the door carefully behind him. Mr. Cowls must have been busy elsewhere, for there was no one in the entry.

No, that wasn't true. She felt the brush against her skirts a moment before she looked down at Fortune. The cat's tail was high, like a flag, as she made another pass.

"I suppose I should thank you too," Abigail said. "Apparently your blessing was required for any of this to happen."

Fortune glanced up as if she was surprised Abigail would have thought otherwise.

The door cracked open, and the cat skittered closer to freedom. But Mr. Huber must have been expecting her, for he maneuvered the door to block her path, then held out his free arm to Abigail. "Ready?"

"Yes," she said, moving around the cat. Fortune appeared to be pouting.

"I think we spoiled her fun," she told him as they started down the street toward busier Park Lane, where he likely meant to hail a hack.

"Lady Belfort warned us she tries to escape," he explained. "We have been careful to prevent it. A small cat would not fare well in all this." His nod took in the passing carriages, the lorry waiting at one of the houses down the way. "Where are we going now?"

"A lodging house off Covent Garden," she said.

She waited for surprise or disdain, but he merely nodded. Perhaps he wasn't cognizant of the areas of

London. He'd know as soon as the carriage turned onto Leary Street.

"I didn't realize you were staying in England," she said as they passed out of the square. "I read in the newspaper that the king's delegation was returning to Batavaria."

"Many of the guards chose to go home," he said, one hand on her elbow as if to steer her through any storm. "Prince Otto Leopold will come back to England after the agreement is signed, to serve as ambassador. His brother elected to stay with his wife in Surrey and take up dog breeding."

The tone in his voice told her the occupation shocked him.

"And what about England made you decide to stay?" she asked.

"I met many people here I could admire." His gaze brushed hers, warm. But surely he hadn't stayed in England because of her. Until she'd appeared at Lady Belfort's, he would have had no way to meet her again. A governess did not spend a great deal of time in Society.

And they generally did not require bodyguards.

They had reached Park Lane, and he raised a hand to signal a passing coach. A few moments later, she had told the coachman her direction and was safely inside. Belatedly she realized that she would be sharing a closed carriage with a gentleman. What secrets might be spilled? Another shiver went through her. *Composure!*

Mr. Huber shut the door and looked through the window at her. "I will ride with the coachman and look for trouble."

Well!

At least that took care of her reputation. Mr. Huber obviously excelled at his work.

But the narrow space felt terribly empty as the coach headed off.

Meredith, Lady Belfort, rose from the sofa after Miss Winchester and Mr. Huber had departed. What an interesting development. Miss Winchester had been such a blessing at the house party this summer that it would be a pleasure to assist her. Meredith knew what it was like to have to start over. And after her earlier struggles in life, she had vowed to help gentlewomen and gentlemen in similar situations.

And then there was Mr. Huber. She had yet to discover why he was so determined to remain in England now that his king, the royal family, and its courtiers had been given the right to return to their native Batavaria. He had not mounted the least argument about guarding Miss Winchester, even though a governess was a far cry from a member of the royal court.

"Mr. Cowls?" she called, and her butler materialized in the doorway as if he had been waiting for any word.

"Your ladyship?" he acknowledged.

"Would you send word to Sir Matthew that I would like to speak with him this afternoon before we travel to Rose Hill? I know how he and Charlotte like unraveling the little mysteries we give them. I believe I have one that is sure to please."

"Well?" Roth demanded when Finn arrived at the Chelsea palace later that afternoon. "Did you find the man stalking the governess?"

Finn had explained the situation when he had briefly met with his comrades in the park across from Lady Belfort's residence on Clarendon Square. Now Roth and the others were gathered in the room they had been using as quarters while the king, his sons, and their courtiers had been leasing the palace. The four of them had been given leave to stay until the lease ended, which was only a week away. Most of the servants had already been dismissed. It hadn't been a bad posting, but the walls held far too much gilding for Finn's taste, and the beds were entirely too soft.

"No," he reported as Roth paused in his packing and Keller and Tanner lounged on their beds. "I watched from Clarendon Square to Miss Winchester's lodging, then stayed in the area a quarter hour. I saw nothing and no one suspicious."

Tanner chuckled. "What did you expect playing bodyguard to a governess?"

Finn refused to stiffen.

"It is a suitable occupation," Roth mused, stroking his clean-shaven chin as if he had considered the matter himself. "And I suppose Lady Belfort's provision of room and board is sufficient pay for the moment."

"Do you think it will be as nice as this?" Keller asked wistfully as he glanced around. Apparently some liked gilt.

"That does not matter," Roth told him. "It is more important that we find positions here to support us. Come, help me carry these trunks to the door so we are ready to leave in the morning."

Keller climbed to his feet and went to oblige.

Tanner watched them go, then tipped up his chin to Finn. "Do you really think Miss Winchester is in danger?"

"She believes so," Finn said, going to finish his own packing. There wasn't much. When the Congress of Vienna had awarded the kingdom of Batavaria to its neighbor, Württemberg, the king, his family, and many of his courtiers had gone into exile. The majority of the Imperial Guards had gone as well. Finn had lived in Italy,

Germany, and now England following his king. He had learned to pack light.

"So you would lower yourself to serve as her bodyguard on a whim?" Tanner demanded.

A sharp retort pressed against his lips. Patience won. He had had to cultivate it over the years. The boy who had been sent to school to learn to serve his country had only wanted to run back to the alpine meadows where he had been raised. But there was no one and nothing there for him. Then, as now, he must look to the future.

"Lady Belfort asked it of me," he said as he tucked his spare pair of boots, shined to Roth's approval, into the trunk. He decided not to mention that he had come to admire the lady's work at the house party.

"Makes you wish you'd returned to Batavaria, eh?" Tanner teased.

"No." Finn turned away to pull another coat from the wardrobe. He had needed only two and a set of evening wear when he'd been a guard with dress uniforms. Now, he supposed, he'd need more.

"No?" Tanner was obviously unwilling to let the matter lie. "You never told me why you did not return to Batavaria. I had thought you a loyal son. You can certainly rhapsodize about the snow, the rivers, the trees."

A wave of longing swept through him. Oh, for one more glimpse of that crystalline sky, one more breath of the crisp, clear air. In London, the buildings crowded so close he struggled to see the clouds. And too often the air was tainted by smoke and other smells.

"I have no future in Batavaria," he told Tanner. "None of us does. That's why we stayed in England."

"True," Tanner allowed. "Though I, for one, was hoping for a little adventure. Perhaps I should ask Lady Belfort to find me a position of bodyguard as well, to such a lovely lady."

Finn eyed him. "And her husband and children."

Tanner barked a laugh. "Very likely. Just my luck."

His luck as well. For the lady he had once loved had been far above him, and no position he could hope to fill would ever have made him a likely suitor for her hand.

Abigail nearly lost her nerve that evening. She'd lived in London all her life. What did she know about the country? It might be sparsely enough populated to keep others from associating her with her father, but wouldn't a sparse population also mean there were few children in need of a governess? She had only viewed Lady Belfort in passing at the party. Could she truly be counted on as an ally? And what of Finn Huber? A bodyguard, like a lady's maid, might be privy to her secrets. Did she want him that close?

Her thoughts were in such turmoil as she stepped outside the lodging house to procure a meat pie from a local vendor for dinner that she didn't notice the man until he stopped directly in front of her. He was short and slight, silvery hair partially covered by a battered cap.

"Wherever you're going," he said, voice as sharp as his narrow-set eyes, "you'd be wise to keep your trap shut."

Abigail blinked, and he darted down a side alley. She stood for a moment, shaking. Keep silent? About what? Everyone knew her father's shame. Why did they insist on making it hers?

The meat pie no longer sounded the least appetizing. She returned to the boardinghouse and attempted to focus on packing.

But everything reminded her of what she'd lost. Three day dresses and a dinner dress were all that remained of her once fashionable wardrobe, and none would be of any use in the coming winter. She'd commissioned the two wool gowns, one grey and one navy, since becoming a governess.

"What need will we have for wool in Poyais?" her mother had said happily as they'd bundled their warmer clothes and coats to be donated to the poor. "The tropics call for cottons and linens. And the wife and daughter of the Royal Banker must look their best."

The Royal Banker. How her father and mother had preened over the title. They had had no way of knowing there was no Bank of Poyais, no royal city, no city at all waiting on the balmy shores, only disease and death.

Composure. She had work to do. She pushed through, as she had been doing for the last two years, and stepped out of the lodging house at eight the next morning, juggling two large satchels and a bandbox.

Only to find a familiar figure on the pavement.

"Mr. Huber?" Before she could do more than state his name, he was moving to take her luggage to store in the hack that stood waiting. "How long have you been here?"

"Shortly after first light," he admitted, returning to fetch her. He was wearing the navy coat again, though his trousers were a serviceable brown and his cravat simply knotted. "I was uncertain when you intended to leave for Lady Belfort's, and I wanted to be on hand to assist. The area is secure. If you will?" He motioned toward the coach.

Bemused, Abigail let him hand her up into it, and they set off. Once more, he rode on the bench with the coachman. She could have wished for his company. Anything to stop the frantic hammering of her heart, which seemed to prefer the confines of London, even with its threats, to an unknown future.

Three coaches were standing before Lady Belfort's door when Abigail alighted on Mr. Huber's arm a short while later. One was a green lacquered affair with silver appointments, surely the family carriage. The other two looked more worn, likely hired for the occasion. She sighted Mr. Tanner peering out of the second carriage. The guards must be taking it. A portly lady and older gentleman were climbing into the third. That must be the coach for the servants. Perhaps she would be expected to ride in it. She must remember she was no longer the daughter of a prominent banker. She was a governess turned companion.

The elderly butler, Mr. Cowls, was issuing orders in his wheezy voice.

"Miss Winchester," he said on spying her. "You will be riding in the coach with her ladyship and Mr. Huber."

A tingle of pleasure went through her. Silly. Lady Belfort had asked her to act as companion, and Mr. Huber was only attending them because his patroness expected it of him.

But as he saw her things stored in the boot, she allowed the waiting footman to hand her in. She had just arranged her skirts on the rear-facing seat when Mr. Huber set the coach to shaking as he climbed up.

"You're not riding with the coachman?" she asked, chiding herself with how breathless she sounded.

"No," he said with a frown. "I can better protect you and Lady Belfort from inside as we leave London. However, that is my seat."

Abigail blinked. "Shouldn't you ride next to her ladyship?"

"And leave you riding backward?"

He made it sound as if she'd asked to journey to Surrey flying on a raven's back.

"I am a servant," she reminded him. "It is our place to ride backward."

"You are a governess," he corrected her. "And a lady who is acting as Lady Belfort's companion." He reached out, seized her by the shoulders, and hefted her up and onto the forward-facing seat.

"Well," Abigail said, righting herself as he plunked her down. "You might ask first."

"I did ask first."

"You ordered first," she pointed out, smoothing down her skirts with hands that persisted in trembling.

He inclined his head. "You are correct. Forgive me. But I will not allow you to inconvenience yourself for me."

"Yet you would inconvenience yourself for me," she protested. "A bodyguard for a governess, of all things!"

"A bodyguard for a lady," Lady Belfort corrected her as the footman handed her in. She settled beside Abigail, arranging her purple-blue redingote around her, then opened her arms, and a maid offered her Fortune. The cat's tail swept back and forth, and her ears were not nearly as high as usual.

"She does not like travel," Lady Belfort explained as if she'd seen Abigail's look. "And she prefers London to the estate. More people to see. Rose Hill will seem particularly empty with Julian gone." She glanced out the window, but not before Abigail noticed her lavender-colored eyes tearing.

"Have you heard from Lord Belfort?" she asked as they all swayed with the carriage's forward motion. Mr. Huber's gaze swung from window to window, watching for any trouble.

"Not as yet," Lady Belfort said, voice catching. "But it is early days, and I doubt they could post a letter until they reached France. Likely we will hear something soon. In the meantime, I intend to keep busy. Besides finding positions for you and the guards, I will need to reacquaint myself with our local families—the Hewetts, Garveys, and Godwins, and of course dear Jane, the Duchess of Wey. I imagine she's feeling a bit at a loose end with the boys back in school and all her daughters now married."

She made it sound as if there were a much larger Society in the country than Abigail had thought. What would she do if one of them truly had invested in the scheme that had cost her father his reputation and ultimately his life?

CHAPTER THREE

THEY REACHED ROSE Hill at noon, having stopped to rest the horses along the way. Miss Winchester gazed out the window as if entranced by the simplicity of the long white-stone house. Finn looked at the recessed double-door flanked by fluted columns and realized it would provide shelter from assailants. If those black shutters around each window could be closed, they might fortify the house. The small garden directly across the circular graveled drive would prove problematic. Too many places to hide. And the ornamental pond was large enough to drown a man.

"What a pretty place," she said as the carriage drew up in front of the door.

Finn climbed down and handed first Lady Belfort and then Miss Winchester down. Mr. Cowls stepped out of the servants' carriage to direct everyone else. He ordered the groomsman driving the carriage with Roth, Keller, and Tanner down a lane to one side, leading through a copse of trees. That must be where the guest cottage lay.

Finn knew his role. He had performed it many times for the prince and king. He marched past the army of servants and into the house.

The entry hall, like the other rooms he toured through, was paneled in squares of dark wood, but someone had taken the trouble to brighten each room with plenty of lamps and pretty hangings and paintings. The ground floor held a Great Hall, library, dining room, and kitchens, the last just filling with servants reacquainting themselves with the house and the staff who had remained behind to manage the place in Lady Belfort's absence. The next floor up had several bedchambers and a withdrawing room. The top floor held rooms for the staff. All were empty of anyone who should not have been there.

"You may enter," he told Lady Belfort and Miss Winchester, who had just gained the entry hall as he came back down the stairs. "There is no danger here."

"There generally isn't," Lady Belfort said, carrying her pet toward the stairs. "But thank you for checking, Mr. Huber."

"Was that necessary?" Miss Winchester whispered to him.

"I vowed to protect you," Finn said. "This is how I do it."

Lady Belfort must have caught the exchange, for she turned with an amused smile. "I believe we are sufficiently safe that you can see to your unpacking for now, Mr. Huber. Return as soon as you are settled, and we can discuss the best way forward."

Something in him wanted to argue, and he wasn't sure why. So, he clapped his fist to his chest, spun on his heels, and marched out.

Grooms and footmen were still unloading the two remaining carriages as he stepped onto the drive. He sucked in a breath of autumn, the air crisp as an apple. The tall leafy trees on either side of the lane leading to the cottage were nothing like the spruce of his native Batavaria, which were strong and stout from weathering alpine winters. These were losing their leaves, speckling the lane with patches of gold and bronze. But he tallied the number of hiding places among them as well as the spots that might provide the best defense.

The lane opened up before a smaller version of the

main house, with a stable off to one side. He would do his fellow soldiers the courtesy of assuming they had already checked it for intruders.

Their belongings had at least been unloaded, for trunks and satchels were piled in the entry hall as Finn stepped through the door. The space was smaller than that at the main house, or perhaps it was the presence of his comrades that filled the hall. From it, he could see the sitting room on this floor as well as a corridor that likely led to the dining room and kitchen.

A younger man was hovering next to the stairs, as if Roth's scowl had pinned him in place. The dark suit and breeches proclaimed him a footman. Finn took pity on the fellow.

"Kind of Lady Belfort to see to our needs," he said, extending a hand. "Finn Huber, formerly of the Imperial Guards. That is Roth, Tanner, and Keller. You will find we require little assistance."

"Yes, sir," he said, head bobbing as much in acknowledgment as relief, Finn thought.

"How many servants did she give us?" Roth asked, looking up from his study of their belongings.

The footman squared his shoulders and stared straight ahead. "Myself; Mrs. Wanrow, the cook; and Maisy, our maid of all work. And I have been trained as a valet, should you need one."

"Doubtful," Roth said, "but you have our thanks. We will carry our things to our quarters. Is there a fire in the hearth in the sitting room?"

"Yes, sir," he said. "And I took the liberty of bringing up coal for the fires in each of the two bedchambers."

"Good," Roth said.

"Good, Mr. …?" Finn pressed.

"Oliver, sir," he said.

"Very good, Oliver," Roth said. "Tell Mrs. Wanrow we will dine at six." He turned to the others. "The rest of you, see to our belongings. Keller, you'll be with me. Tanner and Huber can share."

A short while later, things had been properly sorted. Tanner dropped his satchel on the bed so hard it bounced. "So, this is to be home, is it? Not bad."

Not bad at all. Finn glanced around the room the two of them would be sharing. Like the main house, the walls were paneled in squares of warm wood. A bed stood on either side of the wood-wrapped hearth, their posts, headboards, and footboards of carved mahogany, and their hangings in rose, navy, and spruce. The navy- and spruce-patterned carpet was thick, the chairs by the hearth well-padded. And no gilding in sight. Keller and Roth were sharing a similar bedchamber across the corridor.

Tanner followed his satchel onto the bed, stretching long legs toward the foot. "What do you hope Lady Belfort will find for you, after you're done with the governess?" Of his three comrades, Tanner tended to be the most chatty. He could wish he had been partnered with Keller instead.

"An honorable profession," Finn told him, beginning to move his clothing from the trunk to the wardrobe along one wall. "That is all I ask."

Tanner laced his fingers behind his head. "I would add good pay, a warm bed, and companions to cheer." He winked at Finn. "And of course a pretty lady to woo."

"You will find that while a lady may flirt with an Imperial Guard," Finn told him, shaking out a coat, "she marries a gentleman, preferably with a title."

Tanner rolled his eyes.

Keller poked his blond head through the open doorway. "The sitting room, five minutes. Roth wants a word."

Their self-appointed leader, Roth was pacing before the wood-wrapped hearth when Finn and Tanner entered a few moments later. The black-haired guardsman nodded a greeting, then stopped in front of the glowing fire, feet shoulder's width apart, hands ready at his sides, as Finn and Keller took the two chairs on one side of him.

As if determined to thwart him, Tanner sprawled on the sofa on the other side and crossed his boots at the ankles. Roth's look darkened.

"You wanted us?" Finn reminded him.

"We may be sharing this house for some time," Roth said. "We should reach an understanding."

Tanner cocked an eyebrow. "Are you proposing?"

Roth glowered at him. "At least I take our predicament seriously."

Tanner spread his hands. "Lady Belfort has promised to find us positions. Huber already has work. Until that is true for the rest of us, we have a rare opportunity to enjoy ourselves." He leaned even further back on the sofa and swung his boots up onto the arm.

Roth knocked them off. "Sit up. You are still a soldier. Your commanding officer has merely changed."

Tanner's eyes narrowed. "I do not recall you being promoted."

"He means Lady Belfort," Keller put in. The youngest of the quartet, he tended to play the peacemaker. "She put her reputation at risk by championing us. We must do her proud."

Roth returned to his pacing, wearing a path in the thick blue carpet. "So we must. We must also try not to be a burden to her. We will establish a routine so as not to impose on her ladyship's staff. Breakfast at seven, followed by drills with fist, cutlass, and rifle, then a brisk walk about the estate. Dinner at six, and into quarters by half past eight."

Tanner eyed him, and even Keller was frowning.

"We need not be so regimented," Finn suggested. "I must be at the house most of the day. Someone will need to be there at night. Keller can start. And the rest of us may be required for interviews or to serve as escort to Lady Belfort."

"Point well taken," Roth allowed. "We do not know what sorts of services Lady Belfort will require. Breakfast at seven and dinner as convenient. The drills and walks we can work around our other duties."

"Very well," Finn said. "I will do what I can to determine what those duties might be for the next few days. Keller, would you join me in calling on Lady Belfort? You can set up your space for the night."

"With pleasure." He leapt to his feet. They left Tanner to Roth's questionable graces.

"Can she really do as she promised?" Keller asked as they set off through the wood. Nothing had changed since Finn had passed through, a good sign they were the only ones about.

"I see no reason why not," Finn allowed, boots crunching in the leaves. "Lady Ashforde said Lady Belfort had matched nearly everyone among her friends and family."

Keller shot him a grin. "Actually, she said Fortune had matched nearly everyone," he reminded Finn.

The four of them had recently taken turns guarding Lady Ashforde, the former Petunia, Lady Moselle, when she had been given an assignment from the crown prince: to convince Lord Ashforde to plead their cause with King George to retake their country. Lord Ashforde had indeed sided with them on the matter. The prince had won Batavaria back, and Lord Ashforde had won Lady Moselle.

They had reached the end of the garden, with a clear view down the long, tree-lined drive to the main road. Keller's arm shot out to bar Finn's way, and he jerked his head toward the low, wrought-iron gate at the end. A figure had paused before it, as if to study the house. By the hat and the long coat, Finn thought it was a man.

He purposely put his back to the fellow. "Take the left side. Stay in the trees. We'll flank him."

Keller nodded, then made a show of sauntering across the drive before diving behind a tree. Finn faded back behind the opposite tree.

He wove his way up the drive with every confidence Keller was doing the same. The occasional quick glimpse showed the intruder still watching the house. How many times had he approached an enemy this way during the war? The French and English armies might prefer to march up to each other across a field, but the soldiers of Batavaria had learned to fight in more rugged terrain, where trees and rocks could be allies.

He glanced around the last tree and found the gate empty except for Keller, who was gazing up and down the road that ran from the closest village along the Thames. Disappointment nipped.

"Gone," Keller reported with a sigh. "Perhaps he was merely a local, noting that her ladyship has returned. Here as in Batavaria, people are fascinated by those above them in station."

Finn could only hope that was the reason for the fellow's scrutiny.

"We would be wise to keep watch," he told Keller.

Keller nodded as he fell into step beside him.

The drive at least was clear as they returned to the main house, the carriages and servants gone. Mr. Cowls met them at the door and directed them to the library to wait for Lady Belfort. Finn hadn't expected Miss Winchester to be there before them. She was pulling a book from one of the tall cases.

"Gentlemen," she greeted with a smile. "I trust your accommodations were pleasing."

"Most pleasing," Finn assured her, moving into the room. "You remember Mr. Keller from the other day?"

"Indeed, sir," she said. "And at the house party. You were

very kind to serve in the schoolroom, like Mr. Huber, during the storm."

Keller clapped a fist to his chest. "Always your servant, Miss Winchester."

Finn's cravat felt unaccountably tight, as if someone had tugged on the knot, and he refused to think it had anything to do with the way she beamed at his comrade. He and Keller took seats opposite her on the quartet of leather-bound chairs near the hearth.

Quiet settled. A coal popped in the grate.

"What did you choose to read?" Keller asked politely.

She tipped up the spine and glanced down at it. "Wordsworth. I have always enjoyed his descriptions of the Lakes District. I had hoped to visit it one day."

A governess would not have much opportunity for travel. But Finn knew what she meant about the poet's descriptions.

"'I wandered lonely as a cloud that floats on high o'er vales and hills,'" he quoted from memory. "'When all at once I saw a crowd, a host, of golden daffodils; beside the lake, beneath the trees, fluttering and dancing in the breeze.'"

Her eyes lit. "Oh, well done, sir. That's it entirely." She spared a glance out the window. "Though we won't be spying daffodils this time of year, and Surrey is hardly the Lakes District."

She sounded so wistful he had to ask. "Have you friends or family there?"

"No, indeed," she said. "I spent my life in London, until my parents passed." Her gaze plummeted to the book in her lap as if the memories were too much.

He knew that feeling of devastation, uncertainty. The thought that something fine and good had been taken and could never be recovered.

"It is hard to lose those we count upon," he said. "But

I am sure your mother and father would be proud of the way you are caring for yourself."

"And what of you, Mr. Keller?" she asked perhaps too quickly, turning her face to the other guard. "Have you family still in Batavaria?"

"No, Miss Winchester," he said dutifully. "Most of us were orphans before joining the military. I do not recall my parents."

Her face fell. "Oh, how sad. Was it the same for you, Mr. Huber?"

Those blue eyes were soft, like the sky after a rain.

"I remember my parents and little sister," Finn told her. "They were taken from me when an avalanche swept through our farm."

Her fingers pressed to her lips. "How terrible!"

Her pity knocked loose something he had buried under the snow years ago, that longing for family, the wish that things might be different. To feel one more pat on the shoulder from his father, to hear his little sister's giggle when the butter started to form in the cream, to taste his mother's apple roses set in hot vanilla sauce, every bite imbued with love.

Home had vanished that day, and he had never found its like. His decision to follow his king into exile had limited his ability to return to Batavaria, and his pursuit of a lady had barred the door.

Was it possible he could find a place to call home in this new land?

She had not thought to do more than pass the time politely, but Abigail's heart hurt for the men seated opposite her. She had had both parents growing up. Her mother had been loving, encouraging. Her father had been the voice of reason, always precise in his calculations. How could he have miscalculated so badly the last time?

As if Mr. Keller noted her sorrow, he inched forward on his chair. "Do not weep for us, Miss Winchester. Orphans are not turned out onto the streets in Batavaria as some are here. We attended a boys' school, where the masters worked to give us professions and a future. Mr. Huber was first in his class."

Mr. Huber managed a smile, but she thought it was more for his companion's sake. "You were right behind me, in class and in the army."

"We fought against Napoleon," Mr. Keller explained. "To keep Batavaria safe."

Napoleon had been defeated ten years ago now. She glanced between the two men, so strong in body and temperament. "You must have been boys."

Mr. Huber leaned back in the chair. "I was seventeen. Keller was fifteen."

"Fifteen and a half," Mr. Keller corrected him. He nodded to Abigail. "That is the age a man may enlist in the army during a war in our country."

She shook her head. "You will forgive me, Mr. Keller, but fifteen and a half seems more boy than man to me."

"And yet we were given guns and swords and taught to kill," Mr. Huber said, voice so firm she could not argue. "We were good at it, so good that when the war ended, we were appointed to the highest position any soldier might claim—members of the Imperial Guard."

The silver buttons on Mr. Keller's waistcoat caught the light as his chest swelled. "It was an honor I shall not soon forget."

Lady Belfort came in then, and the two guards stood until she had been seated in the remaining chair. Fortune followed, but instead of hopping up into her mistress' lap, she set about winding around the gentlemen's boots. Her purr reverberated through the room.

"Gentlemen," Lady Belfort said. "Is the cottage to your liking?"

"It is quite comfortable," Mr. Huber assured her. "Thank you for providing staff to see to its care."

"And ours," Mr. Keller added.

She inclined her head. "It is the least I can do after relocating you all."

"And the least we can do is to put ourselves at your disposal," Mr. Huber said. "As Miss Winchester's bodyguard, I will be with you from breakfast to dinner, longer should you go out in the evening. The others will take turns spending the night in the house. You have a room near yours where they may stay?"

"I do," Lady Belfort acknowledged. "You think such tactics necessary?"

Abigail certainly hoped not, but he spread his hands. "Until we know no one has followed us from London and no danger exists here, it would seem to be for the best."

"Very well, then," Lady Belfort allowed. "Do what you must."

"And how might the rest of us be of service?" Mr. Keller asked, eyes bright. He reminded Abigail of a pup a neighbor had owned—such eager devotion.

Lady Belfort smiled. "Tomorrow, you all will join me for church in the village. I want to make sure everyone in the area has a good look at you. And I expect the reception to be outstanding."

CHAPTER FOUR

MR. HUBER WAS as devoted as he'd promised. After Mr. Keller left, he took up a position in one corner of the library while Lady Belfort composed letters at the desk. Having been given no other tasks, Abigail kept her company. That was what companions did, after all, though she began to think she should have a conversation with her ladyship as to duties. Sitting about was a sure way to ruminate, which was not conducive to maintaining her composure.

And either watching Mr. Huber or being watched wasn't helping.

"You needn't stand," she told him when it became apparent he would not return to his chair. "Surely we would be safe if you were to be seated."

"I prefer to stand," he said, gaze on the middle distance.

Lady Belfort glanced up. "It is the habit of the Batavarian Imperial Guards. They generally stood in a corner or along a wall when attending their sovereign."

He had too much life to stand like a statue. And she and Lady Belfort were hardly royalty requiring such attentions. "You sat in the schoolroom," she pointed out to him.

"Because everyone sat, and I did not want to frighten the children," he said as if speaking to the case of books opposite him. "From this vantage point, I can see the window, through the door down the corridor, and to the back of the room."

"Very wise," Lady Belfort commented, her pen slashing through the air as she must have signed a letter with a flourish.

Abigail could not like the habit. It was one thing to keep her safe. It was another to treat him as if he were a piece of furniture, built for her comfort.

"I must insist that Mr. Huber join us for dinner," she said that night when she and Lady Belfort met in the green and gold dining room. Abigail had retired to her room to change, even though she only had her yellow silk gown suitable for evening wear. She had exited her room, just down the corridor from Lady Belfort's, to find the guard and Fortune awaiting her. Both had accompanied her down the stairs.

Fortune had promptly dived under the long white tablecloth, but Mr. Huber had taken up a position from which he could likely see the door to the house, the door to the servant's area, the window, and the entire room.

Lady Belfort eyed him now from her place at the head of a table that could seat eight. "She has a point, Mr. Huber. Nowhere in your schedule did you say when you would be eating."

That firm jaw worked, as if he were struggling with the words. Finally, he nodded. "Very well."

He pulled out a chair across from Abigail, and the footman hurried to set him a place.

"Much better," Lady Belfort commented when he had been served some of the baked smelt, potatoes and leeks, and salad with endive and watercress. "Don't you agree, Miss Winchester?"

"I do," Abigail said, offering him a smile.

He inclined his head. "Thank you both. I will not take advantage of your kindness. As soon as I have eaten, I will resume my position."

He proceeded to shovel the food into his mouth as if he couldn't wait.

Something soft brushed her skirts. Fortune, on the hunt for any offerings.

Lady Belfort returned to her smelt. "If we are to spend so much time together, I think it would behoove us to use our first names. I am Meredith. May I call you Abigail?"

Her cheeks warmed. "I'd be honored, your ladyship."

She arched a dark brow.

"Meredith," Abigail corrected herself. "But I shall call you Lady Belfort in company."

"And what may we call you, Mr. Huber?" Meredith asked.

He swallowed his mouthful of potatoes. "Ho, Guard?"

Abigail stifled a giggle.

Meredith shook her head. "That will not do at all. I seem to recall your first name is Finn."

"It is," he allowed. "Though few use it."

Abigail could not keep silent. "May we?"

His gaze met hers. Something was simmering in the golden brown, but she could not be sure what. Again he inclined his head.

Pleasure whispered through her, but she inwardly shouted it down. He was her bodyguard for the moment. She should not expect more.

Yet as they ate, she could not help remembering their time together at the Duke and Duchess of Wey's house party. A gale had blown up, confining everyone to the castle, and all the guests had graciously taken turns helping her in the schoolroom so the children would not be frightened by the roar around the sturdy stone building.

Lord Thalston and Lord Peter had been her charges, along with Rose and Daphne, the young daughters of Sir Matthew and Lady Bateman. Finn had come in with the prince, his then fiancée and her youngest sister, and

Sir Matthew's sister. The royal family had even sent up Dolph, a big mountain dog, who had stretched out by the fire, eyes sleepy.

Hoping to entertain the children, she had requested that the prince tell them about Batavaria. His smile had proven his delight in sharing the wonders of his homeland.

"Batavaria is a rugged country, bordered by mountains that reach to the sky and rivers that run cold and fast," he'd started.

Miss Daphne Bateman, the youngest in the set at only six, had interrupted him. "Who are they running away from?"

The prince blinked, and the ladies in attendance turned away, smiles tugging.

"No one," he assured the little girl. "Batavarians are very brave, even our rivers."

Lord Peter, the eight-year-old son of the duke, raised his hand and spoke when the prince glanced his way. "How many Batavarians are there?"

"Several thousand," the prince assured him.

"How many are boys?" Lord Peter persisted.

"How many are girls?" Miss Bateman the elder countered with a frown to the lad.

"How many have dogs?" her sister threw in.

"Mr. Huber is also from Batavaria," the prince said, glancing at Finn with a look of panic, as if he were facing Napoleon's troops alone.

Finn sat taller, setting the candlelight glinting on the gilt braid across his chest. "I would be happy to talk about my country, to those who will listen."

A masterful move she could not help but admire. The children quieted, the little girls settling back in their seats. Lord Peter's look was worshipful.

Finn lowered his voice and leaned closer to them. "We have mountains, yes, and rivers, but Batavaria is more than that. It is the cool wind on your face as you climb, the taste of creamy cheese from cows raised on mountain pastures, the sound of church bells calling everyone to worship."

For a moment, she was certain she could hear the bells tolling.

"We have wind," Miss Bateman told him solemnly.

"You can hear it outside," her sister agreed.

"I hear your wind outside," he promised them. He patted the chest of his uniform. "But I hear the wind of Batavaria here, in my heart."

She had been able to keep silent no longer. "Beautifully said, Mr. Huber," she had murmured, and she was fairly certain Lord Peter hadn't been the only one to look worshipful.

At that time, she'd hoped her association with the scandal forgotten. No one had pressed her about the matter in months. She had not thought to see him again after the house party had ended. She certainly hadn't expected to find him at her side as a bodyguard!

But she could not afford to admire him like that again. They were each moving toward a future where entanglements could only hurt. And he did not deserve to be tarred by the scandal she had inherited.

She told herself to be glad that he excused himself after dinner. Mr. Keller took his place. Meredith did not request to use his first name, and the shy blond seemed content to stand along the wall in the library, which appeared to be one of her ladyship's favorite rooms.

Abigail could not feel as contented. After two years of making her own way, constantly expecting reprisal for her father's failings, sitting about felt wrong, as if she were a sailing ship becalmed.

"And what role do you expect me to play in your household?" she ventured as they sat before a glowing fire. "I know some companions help their lady with dressing or correspondence. You do not seem to require aid with either."

Meredith ran a hand along Fortune's fur as the cat dozed in her lap. "I generally have a number of plans moving forward at any time: finding positions for the Imperial Guards and you, ensuring the estate is ready for winter with Julian gone, reestablishing myself in the neighborhood. Feel free to offer suggestions and support. Mostly, however, I would simply like company. I am too used to having my husband beside me."

She'd envisioned such a future for herself once. Her and Preston, sitting like this before a fire, children on their laps as she read. Odd that the fellow in the picture now wore gold braid across his chest.

———————

Meredith had said she wanted everyone to get a good look at the four guards and Abigail, and she received exactly that Sunday morning. Abigail had never been so ogled, from the moment the carriage and wagon rolled onto the streets. Mr. Roth and Finn were inside the carriage with her and Meredith; Mr. Tanner and Mr. Keller were on the roof with the coachman. The household staff rode in the wagon behind.

People on their way to services, dressed in their Sunday best, stopped to stare as they passed. Merchants came out of the doors of their closed establishments to knuckle their foreheads or bow. Even the gravestones in the cemetery in front of the little church seemed to lean toward them as they all started for the chapel.

Finn stayed by Abigail's elbow, gaze swinging over the crowds. She could see nothing of danger to herself among the smiling faces, the bowing heads.

But she certainly saw a danger to him.

The village of Weyton, she knew from her fortnight

with the duke and duchess, was beholden to His Grace for patronage. She had heard the population was close to one hundred. Apparently at least thirty of them were unwed females, for there was an unwarranted number of looks flashing their way, all aimed at Finn and his comrades.

"Lady Belfort! How delightful to have you with us again!" A plump matron blocked their way forward on the flagstone path. The two younger ladies pasted to her back were apparently her daughters, if the color of their blond crimped hair and pale blue eyes were any indication. All wore fashionable gowns bestrewn with lace and trim, making Abigail feel like silver against gemstones in her grey wool.

"Mrs. Bee, Miss Bee, Miss Angelica Bee," her ladyship acknowledged. She attempted to pass, but the lady's bulk shifted, preventing anyone else from moving forward.

"You must make me known to your guests," she said, heavy face bright below her plumed hat. "Such distinguished gentlemen! Friends of your good husband?"

She made a show of glancing about as if Lord Belfort might pop up from behind a gravestone and wave at them.

"This is inappropriate," Mr. Keller murmured to Finn.

"We are too much in the open," Mr. Roth agreed.

"Pardon me," Finn said, wedging his shoulder between Meredith and Mrs. Bee.

The lady was so startled she scuttled back, forcing a squeak out of one of the daughters as they picked up their skirts to avoid the crush.

Mr. Tanner led Meredith and Abigail through the breach.

"Ladies," Finn said with a tip of his hat before following.

Abigail thought she heard a huff behind them.

The church inside was partially lit by stained glass windows, with walnut box pews on either side of a center aisle. The first three boxes on the left had gilded finials and the House of Wey's unicorn crest on the half-doors.

Lady Belfort apparently had her own pew, for she sailed to one near the front of the chapel to the right and took her spot behind the door. Abigail sat beside her. The Imperial Guards overfilled the remaining space, pressing her up against Finn. She smiled an apology.

He kept his gaze forward, but his cheeks were turning pink.

She tried not to notice the number of looks directed their way as the services commenced. Yet it was impossible not to notice him. Finn held the prayer book for her, his large hands cradling the worn leather. His warm voice joined hers in the responses. He nodded at a point the minister made in his sermon, and his shoulder brushed hers. She had to force herself to attend to what the minister was saying.

The moment services ended, they were once more besieged by well-wishers and acquaintances of her ladyship. If Abigail stood a little too close to Finn, it was only to make his job in guarding her easier.

Truly.

Finn kept a hand on Abigail's elbow, cataloging every person who approached. Two young ladies seeking to further their acquaintance with Lady Belfort, hands fluttering. The minister welcoming her back to the parish. Another older woman with daughters. How many did this area boast? He could feel their gazes, like wolves watching a calf. If he stepped too far from his herd...

"Meredith!"

The crowds parted as the Duchess of Wey came forward, her tall husband at her back. Finn, Tanner, Keller, and Roth clapped their fists to their chests in salute. The duke waved them to be at their leisure.

"I didn't know you planned to come home," the duchess said after giving Lady Belfort—impossible to think of her as Meredith even though he had promised—a hug. He knew the duchess had been born and raised in England, and she had darker coloring than the ladies he had associated with growing up, but Finn saw much of Batavaria in that sturdy figure and confident smile.

"With Julian away, it seemed wise," Lady Belfort said. "And I have work. You remember the Imperial Guards?"

"Mr. Huber, Mr. Keller, Mr. Roth," she said with smiles all around. That smile broadened when she glanced at his friend. "And Mr. Tanner. I hope you have no more need to play spy."

Tanner had been on outpost duty on their last visit. Instead of attending the house party, he had ridden about the area, keeping an eye out for trouble. And he had found it.

"No spying, Your Grace," he assured her. "I leave that to Huber this trip."

She raised her dark brows. "Expecting to repel boarders, Mr. Huber?"

His grip on Abigail's elbow tightened. "If I must, Your Grace."

She laughed. "Good man."

"Good men," Lady Belfort corrected her. "I am seeking positions for all of them. You don't happen to know of any?"

Roth straightened. Keller tugged down on his waistcoat. Tanner gave the duchess his best smile. There was no shame in working for a duke, in any position.

"Alas, no," she admitted, and Keller sagged. "But I'll keep my ears open. If you need a letter of recommendation, we'd be happy to write one, for any of the guards."

They all thanked her for that.

"And Miss Winchester," the duchess said, turning her

way. "What a pleasure to see you again. Who was clever enough to hire you?"

"I was," Lady Belfort said before Abigail could answer. "She is serving as my companion while Julian is away. You must come visit us, Jane, and we can catch up."

"I'll be by as soon as possible," Her Grace promised.

"Did I hear these men require positions?" the minister asked, joining them again and beaming around. "I'm sure there must be some in our area."

Others were nodding.

"Send any ideas my way," Lady Belfort instructed them. "These men were members of the elite Batavarian Imperial Guards. They are highly skilled in protection and instruction. Whoever chooses to hire them will be fortunate indeed. Gentlemen, Miss Winchester."

She breezed through the crowds, and Finn angled his body to keep it between Abigail and the others as they followed. Roth was being as careful, handing Lady Belfort into the carriage and handing her out again when they reached Rose Hill.

"Watch over them," he murmured to Finn before turning to her ladyship and holding up a hand to stop her and Abigail from entering the house. "Was everyone attending services this morning, Lady Belfort?"

"Except for a maid who was feeling poorly," she said with a frown. "Fortune stayed with her."

"Then wait here, until I determine it is safe." He turned, shoved through the door, and disappeared.

"I begin to regret I asked for your help," Lady Belfort said. Her foot must have been tapping, for her skirts swung with the movement.

"It is only to ensure your safety," Finn promised her, though his gaze persisted in brushing Abigail's. "That is what you asked me to do."

"And do you think to find a villain hiding in my

home?" her ladyship demanded. "We have been gone no more than two and a half hours, and most of those in the area were with us the majority of the time."

"*Most* of those in the area," Finn said.

Abigail sent him a commiserating look before turning to their patroness. "What else did you have planned for today, Meredith?"

Lady Belfort's frown did not ease, but at least her foot had stopped tapping. "Tomorrow, I have meetings with our bailiff and others who remained behind while we were in London. I will also meet with the Imperial Guards about next steps. But today, I had hoped to write to my husband, though heavens knows when he will receive it. And I planned to write to other acquaintances in Surrey about possible positions."

"I am certain Finn and the others would not want to slow that process," Abigail said with another look his way.

Every time she said his first name, something uncurled inside him, like Fortune stretching after a long nap. He refused to allow it to be his heart awakening. The last time it had become involved, he had regretted it. And so had the man he had nearly maimed.

Roth appeared in the doorway. "You may enter. Huber, a word."

Lady Belfort brushed past him, head high. With another glance at Finn, Abigail followed.

"What did you find?" Finn asked him.

Roth closed the distance between them, steely eyes intent. "The rear door was unlocked. Nothing appears to have been stolen, but I cannot like such a lapse in security. We must make sure nothing happens to her ladyship or Miss Winchester. We will none of us find positions if we cannot keep our ladies safe. Our honor is at stake."

CHAPTER FIVE

AND SO THEY upheld their honor. At times, Finn wondered whether that was all they possessed, aside from a few changes of clothing, their shaving tools, and their weapons. Most of them had gone from school or labor to war to the Guard. Even considering there might be more to life was something new, intangible, fragile.

He remained on duty that afternoon and evening, but he saw and heard nothing that might concern him. Tanner came to sleep in the house that night. Before Finn left, he was already seated beside Abigail and Lady Belfort and engaging in conversation, as if he were a guest rather than a guard. The urge to knock some sense into that chestnut head was almost overpowering.

He must remember that Tanner knew what he was about, despite his teasing manner. Yet he felt as if fingers tugged at his coattails, pulling him back toward the house, as he trudged for the cottage in the moonlight.

"Report," Roth demanded as Finn stepped inside.

Finn raised his brows at the sight of the older guardsman standing in the doorway to the sitting room, arms crossed over his chest.

"Nothing," Finn said. "No sign of any danger."

Roth nodded. "Then we will sleep."

He wasn't ready to let the matter go in the morning either, for he inspected Finn and Keller before allowing them to take the short walk to the house. Finn was to start his duties for the day, and the others were to meet with Lady Belfort. Roth nodded approval to Finn's navy coat and fawn trousers, the uniform so many London gentlemen effected. But he stopped in front of Keller and scowled.

"What," he drawled, "is that about your neck?"

Keller's fingers brushed at the knot of red and yellow-flecked silk. "A cravat called the Belcher."

Roth cocked his head. "And what would her ladyship or any of her acquaintances want with a fellow who belches?"

"Belcher is the name of one of their pugilists," Finn supplied. "Lady Moselle told me of him. A giant of a man, well respected."

Roth straightened. "Very well. I will allow it. Right face. March."

Keller sighed in obvious relief before following Roth and Finn out the door.

Sunlight filtered through the trees as they marched along the lane, boots thudding on the damp earth. Their reflections rippled across the water of the pond as they passed. A bird swooped by, and another called from the wood. For a moment, he could almost imagine himself back in Batavaria.

"Halt!" Roth commanded as they reached the front door to Lady Belfort's residence. He rapped sharply on the panel.

Mr. Cowls opened the door and regarded them balefully.

"Roth, Huber, and Keller," Roth barked at him. "Reporting as requested by her ladyship. Tanner should be on duty."

The butler shuffled aside to let them in, then nodded to the stairs. "The withdrawing room off the first landing, if you please. Her ladyship is expecting you. Mr. Tanner is with her."

Their steps echoed against all the wood paneling as they climbed the stairs.

Dressed in her usual lavender, Lady Belfort was waiting for them in a room decorated in rose and grey. As if Abigail knew the weather was too cool for her pretty summer gown embroidered with daisies, she'd draped a shawl over her shoulders.

Finn made sure not to sit too close, choosing a hard-backed chair near the window, where he could keep watch.

And if the spot gave him an excellent view of the light playing across her sleek hair, that was merely an accident. Fortune, on the sill beside him, sent him a knowing look.

Roth remained standing. Keller quickly took a seat, as if securing himself a place before Roth could protest.

"I trust all is well with you," Lady Belfort said, glancing around at them.

"Quite well," Roth answered with a look to Tanner, who was already seated. "No trouble yesterday afternoon or last night?" He glanced at Abigail.

She smiled. "None whatsoever, Mr. Roth. I could not have asked for better protection than Mr. Huber and Mr. Tanner."

Finn inclined his head. Tanner grinned.

Fortune dropped from the sill and started forward, only to pull up short in front of Roth. She nudged one boot with her head. Roth did not so much as glance down, keeping his gaze on Lady Belfort.

"I have been giving the matter of your positions considerable thought," she said. "You have several options open to you."

Fortune wound back and forth between Roth's legs. The senior guardsman's jaw tightened.

Abigail must have noticed his torture, for she dropped her hand and wiggled her fingers. Fortune disdained the invitation. Abandoning Roth's boots, she meandered closer to Keller. He bent as if to pet her, and Roth shook his head once, hard. Keller straightened.

"Such as?" Tanner asked.

"A tutor for one," Lady Belfort said as if unaware of her pet's antics. "A number of noblemen want men trained in swordplay to teach their sons the art of the blade."

"Keller, then," Roth said. "He is the best."

Keller's color deepened. "I would be honored to pass along what I know."

Once again, Abigail attempted to coax Fortune closer, running her fingers up and down the skirts of her embroidered cotton gown. How could the cat resist? Finn would have been venturing closer to see if those slender fingers were as supple as they seemed. He could imagine them threading through his hair.

He sat straighter than Keller.

Fortune moved on to Tanner, who wiggled his foot just enough to set the tassel on his boot to swinging. Fortune watched it, arrested.

"There's also the possibility of taking the role of a bodyguard, as Mr. Huber is currently serving," her ladyship continued. "Lord Worthington, Lady Bateman's brother, originally hired Sir Matthew, when he was the Beast of Birmingham, to serve as such. There are likely others seeking similar services."

Sir Matthew Bateman had saved the life of the then-prince regent and been awarded a baronetcy for his trouble. He had also been, for a time, considered the bare-knuckle champion of England. All of the Imperial Guards looked on him with admiration.

"We would make excellent bodyguards," Roth assured her.

Fortune launched herself at Tanner's boot, and he barely managed to swivel away in time. She skittered out of sight under his chair.

"Except perhaps Tanner," Roth amended with a dark look to their comrade.

"Finally," Lady Belfort said, "certain merchants require guards to protect their property. Some hire older men, but I believe some may be open to younger gentlemen, well skilled. Regrettably, many would see this as quite a step down from your former profession."

Fortune reappeared next to Finn and glanced up at him as if to gauge how he would respond. He bent and ran his fingers along the silky fur. She leaned into his hand with a contented purr. Roth glowered at him. Finn ignored him.

Miss Winchester beamed at him as if he'd done something fine and courageous. It was impossible not to smile back.

"Mr. Keller," Lady Belfort said, "I will give you the direction of Mr. Frances Haymaker. He would like to speak to you about a position tutoring at his boys' school across the river from Hampton Court. Mr. Roth, Mr. Thackery in the village is seeking a night guard for his steam works. I will give you both a letter of recommendation. Mr. Huber, Mr. Tanner, I will see what I can find for you in the coming days."

Roth bowed to the two ladies. Keller and Tanner rose and did likewise, with a more expansive gesture from the latter.

"Secure the house," Roth ordered Finn.

Finn stood and inclined his head to Abigail and Lady Belfort before following the others out.

"She favors you," Tanner said as they started down the stairs, Keller and Roth ahead of them.

"I saw no indication that Lady Belfort favors any of us," Finn told him.

Tanner bumped him with his shoulder. "Not Lady Belfort. Miss Winchester."

Warmth curled through him at the thought. No! He would not allow it. "I saw no indication of that either."

"Then you weren't looking," Tanner declared. "She only had eyes for you. And the cat."

"Very likely it was only the cat," Finn said.

"You are too humble, my friend." Tanner spread his arms as they reached the entry hall. "Embrace what life offers you!"

"Life has, thus far, offered me a profession and companions worthy of it," Finn allowed. "And I am grateful."

Roth stopped them all at the door. "Tanner, walk the perimeter with Huber to ensure all is well. Keller and I will prepare for our interviews."

Tanner managed to refrain from rolling his eyes until Roth and Keller were out the door. He and Finn then set out on a circuit of the grounds closest to the house.

Contrary to its name, Rose Hill was situated on more of a slight rise, with fields closest to the house giving way to woods beyond. From their time at the duke's castle, Finn knew the Thames to be less than a mile to the north. The drive out to the road remained clear, the wrought-iron gate securely closed.

"There is nothing here to disturb anyone," Tanner declared. He bent, scooped up a handful of leaves and tossed them into the air, where they fluttered down. "We are free."

Odd. Finn didn't feel free. He tugged his coat closer.

Tanner cast him a sidelong glance as they rounded the back of the house and the garden that stretched out, beds still showing evidence of hardier vegetables and herbs. "Do you truly see danger here?"

"No," Finn admitted. "But we would be wise to be on our guard."

Tanner sighed. "We are always on our guard. That has been our role. Perhaps I want more adventure than marching before the king during court ceremonies and watching from the wall while anything interesting happens. You, however, seem content to watch from the wall. Why forego the pleasure? Why not return to Batavaria with the prince?"

If he was going to confide in any of his friends, Tanner seemed the least likely. He talked too much, and, as Roth had noted, he seemed to take little seriously. Yet memories had been tormenting him lately. Would it help to tell another, at least the bare outline?

"Do you remember Lady Giselle?" Finn asked as they ducked under an arbor where fat red grapes dangled.

"Daughter of the Count of Gourtier?" Tanner clarified. "Who could forget? Those golden tresses, those pouty lips." He eyed the cloudy sky and sighed theatrically.

Irritation quickened Finn's steps. "She offered me her favor."

Tanner jerked to a stop, staring at him. When Finn stopped as well, he whistled. "Oh, well done. But of course you refused."

Finn rubbed the back of his neck, which felt as if the sunlight had speared through the trees to heat it with fire.

Tanner's eyes widened. "Oh, ho! You accepted. Why have I not attended a wedding?"

Finn dropped his hand. "Because her father made it clear that her favors are not for the likes of me."

"And did you tell her father where he might shove those old-fashioned ideas?" Tanner demanded, face darkening.

"No," Finn said, moving forward again and forcing Tanner to keep pace. "Because he was right. What have I to offer a lady of her station? I have no estate, no noble name, no peerless lineage."

"You are a respected member of the Imperial Guard," Tanner protested. "You know what that's worth in Batavaria."

"We weren't in Batavaria," Finn reminded him as they headed for the front of the house again. "We were in Italy at the time, with no idea of when we might return home. She was persuaded to see her father's side of the matter, and I was persuaded not to fight for her."

That wasn't all of the sorry tale, but he hoped it would be enough to satisfy Tanner. Every time Finn thought of what might have happened when he'd put love over duty, his stomach roiled. Lady Giselle's brother had come within an inch of his life, because of Finn's inattention.

Tanner lay a hand on his shoulder, pulling him up short. "She did not deserve you to fight for her if she was so easily dissuaded, my friend. Save your love for a lady who values it enough to fight for you too." He clapped his hand on Finn's shoulder before withdrawing it. "I understand our maid Maisy has a sister. That is, if Miss Winchester proves as fickle as Lady Giselle."

Abigail turned from the window with a smile. Whatever Mr. Tanner had said to Finn, it had put a scowl on his face even as Tanner grinned. For a moment, they reminded her of Lord Thalston and Lord Peter, the duke's sons, boys moving into manhood.

Only there was no doubt in her mind that Finn Huber was a man.

"You are restive," Meredith commented. "Perhaps a walk while the weather holds?"

"I would not dream of inconveniencing you and Fortune," Abigail said, returning to her seat near the hearth. "And it appears to require an armed guard when I so much as move from one room to the next."

Meredith chuckled. "He is very protective of you. I find that commendable."

The sound of a door below was followed by the thump

of boots on the stairs. Abigail caught herself watching the door. Fortune must have been doing the same, for she ran to greet Finn as he stepped into the room.

He glanced from Meredith to Abigail, who put on a smile. Then he marched to his usual spot and took up his place along the wall.

Abigail sighed.

Meredith stood. "That is entirely enough of that. I have an appointment with my bailiff this afternoon. For now, we are going into Weyton. Finn, see that the carriage is brought around. And you will be riding inside, with us."

What her ladyship wanted, her ladyship received. Abigail couldn't mind. She asked Meredith questions about the various houses and farms they passed, while Finn sat across from them, gaze watching the road as if he expected them to meet highwaymen around every curve.

Tidy, whitewashed cottages announced the start of the village. Beyond the church, she spotted a blacksmith, cooper, dry goods merchant, and baker.

"And that is new," Meredith mused as the carriage pulled up before the post office. She nodded to a shop across the street, which proclaimed itself to belong to a linen draper. "Shopping, in Weyton. A sign of progress."

The only other sign of progress was the number of carriages pulled up around the inn along the river. It seemed many people had found reason to visit the little village.

"All passing through," the postmaster assured them when Meredith asked for her mail and mentioned the throng. "Some going shooting out at one of the country estates." A white-haired fellow with brawny arms, he plopped the sack down on the counter. "We forwarded some to you in London, my lady, but this is the lot that's come through in the last two weeks along with some local notes from today. Some of our neighbors have thoughts on what to do with your guards." He nodded to Finn.

"Thank you, Mr. Summers," Meredith said with a winning smile. She looked to Finn, who helpfully took up the sack.

"Fellow came looking for you too," the postmaster threw out.

Finn stiffened. "Looking for whom?"

"Her ladyship, of course," he said, puffing out his chest as if much miffed at being questioned. "Short older man, squinty eyes. I didn't like the look of him. I sent him out with a flea in his ear, I can promise you."

Immediately, the man who had warned her in London the last night sprang to her mind. He had certainly been short and older, and his eyes might have been considered to squint. But he hadn't seemed to know where she was going. If he had somehow followed her to Weyton, why ask after Meredith instead?

"Thank you, Mr. Summers," Meredith said again. "I can always count on the people of Weyton to see to my best interests."

"Well, of course, your ladyship," he said with a grin. "We remember when you were little Mary Rose."

She paled, but her smile was polite as she left him.

Mary Rose? She was certain Lady Belfort's maiden name was Thorn. Perhaps Abigail wasn't the only one with a past she'd prefer to forget.

<hr>

Meredith had long ago mastered the ability to say nothing, with force. So she wasn't surprised when neither her new companion nor her guard broached the subject of the name she had hoped never to hear again. A shame others could not forget.

When they returned to the house, she used the excuse of needing to see to the mail and asked Abigail to exercise Fortune in the yard. Her pet hated her jeweled collar and leash, but it was the only way to keep her safe, particularly when their country estate had so very many places where she could hide.

She retired to the library and thumbed through the letters but failed to find that elegant hand she so longed to see. Disappointment sat on her shoulders like a sodden cloak. But wait, there was a masculine slash she seemed to recall seeing before. Opening it, she found that Sir Matthew had been busy on her behalf.

"Looked into Miss Winchester's former employer, Lord Granbury," he'd written. "Seemed a decent chap. Was willing to meet with me at any rate. He claims he doesn't know why Miss Winchester left his employ. She gave his good wife no reason except that the position did not suit her. The employment agency had no knowledge of her whereabouts. He was sorry to have lost her and offered to raise her salary if I could find and return her to him."

Interesting. She wasn't surprised that his lordship would seek to rehire Abigail. Sir Matthew's wife, Charlotte, spoke so glowingly of the governess's abilities. Yet Abigail had said he'd made things unpleasant for her.

"There's another oddity as well," the letter continued. "I checked at the lodging house in Covent Garden to see if anyone else had come looking for her. Mrs. Pepperman, the owner, said a man had come calling, but refused to give his name. I have his description, but it's common enough I'm not likely to identify him. Be on your guard. I'll write if I learn more."

Meredith lay down the note. Abigail had mentioned

a scandal with her father. It very much sounded as if she had lost her place in Society as a result or surely she wouldn't have become a governess. Who, then, had come seeking her? A brother, looking to mend fences? A beau, hoping to offer a different future than being in service?

Or a villain, looking for prey?

CHAPTER SIX

ABIGAIL HAD NEVER seen a leash for a cat before, but she had a feeling the gemstones winking in Fortune's collar would have funded a London Season. The cat did not seem to care. She twisted and rubbed her neck against the bushes, sending leaves fluttering onto the graveled path.

"Why did Lady Belfort send us out?" Finn asked at Abigail's side. He looked no more pleased than the cat, studying the rear garden as if wondering what it was hiding.

"This is a pretense," she told him as they followed the cat along the paths. "Meredith wanted to go through the mail alone."

He frowned at her. "Why? Is someone blackmailing her?"

Abigail blinked. "Heavens no! At least, I cannot think it likely."

"She changed her name," he pointed out.

So, he'd come to the same conclusion about the postmaster's comment. "Women change their names when they marry. Perhaps Mary is short for Meredith and Rose is her maiden name."

"Perhaps," he said, but he did not sound convinced.

"Is it a requirement of your position that you expect the worst of everyone?" she asked as they came around a bed of herbs, the air scented with mint. Fortune stopped to sniff at the plants.

"It should be," he said. "One of the ways a bodyguard protects is to look for any possible difficulties." He nodded to a pear tree on their right, the boughs still heavy with fruit. "Is that branch weak enough to fall on us as we pass? Could someone be hiding behind the trunk?"

She would never maintain her composure if she looked at the world that way!

A finch burst out of a rose bush. Fortune lunged across the path in pursuit, pulling the leash taut against Abigail's skirts. She stumbled, tumbled.

Strong arms caught her and held her gently.

Her heart beat faster than the wings of the fleeing bird as she gazed into Finn's eyes. So close, she could see every golden fleck in the brown.

"And sometimes," he murmured, "we fail to see the danger. Then we can only react and hope for the best."

His breath brushed her cheek. She had never been kissed, but she could imagine those lips brushing hers as gently. Something flickered in his eyes, as if he imagined it too.

The tug on her wrist reminded her of her duty. At least she had not allowed Fortune to escape. She managed to get her feet under her, and he helped her to stand upright.

Fortune looked her way as if to demand that they follow the bird.

"Time to return to the house, I think," Abigail told her.

Before her thoughts betrayed her.

Finn tried to focus on his duty, but Abigail's tumble in the garden kept popping back into his mind the rest of the afternoon and evening. He had caught her close merely to protect her from a fall, but the feel of her in his arms, the way her gaze had clung to his lips as if she hoped for a kiss, had raised an answering longing in him. What was wrong with him? He was supposed to be looking for danger, not causing it, to her or to himself.

So, he ruthlessly forced his mind to action and asked Tanner the next morning to watch over the ladies, borrowed a horse from Lady Belfort's stable, and rode in to the village. The postmaster's comment about a stranger asking questions concerning Lady Belfort had left Finn with an unsettled feeling, as if he hadn't put on a sword before a battle. Best to run that rumor to ground.

By definition, a true stranger to the area would not be staying with any of the local families. That would have made the fellow a relative or an acquaintance, if only on the thinnest of connections. Perhaps the innkeeper could tell him more about a man unknown to any.

The low, slate-roofed inn perched along the Thames to the east of the island that held the duke's castle. Like Lady Belfort's home, the public room was paneled in wood, but the dark wood tables and chairs made it seem more like a cavern. He counted five men enjoying the space—a trio of farmhands, based on their smocks, near the hearth, steaming cups before them; a fellow in the tailored clothing of a gentleman, tucking into a breakfast of eggs and sausage; and a man in a rougher coat, sitting in the corner, watching Finn as closely as Finn watched him.

A tall, thin man stood behind the high counter that divided the main room from the kitchens, drying metal tankards with a rag. Finn approached and nodded a greeting.

"Here for breakfast?" the barkeep asked, eyeing Finn's coat as if attempting to determine its quality, and his.

"No, thank you," Finn replied in a quieter tone. "I had hoped for information. I serve Lady Belfort, and I understand a stranger has been asking questions about her. I thought perhaps he might be staying here."

"Great many people staying the last few days," he said, peering down into the tankard as if to spy every last drop of water. "But I think you may be after *that* fellow." He nodded toward the corner.

Of course.

Finn thanked him and strolled in that direction. The man watched every step, eyes narrowed. They were more protruding than squinty, and even though the man was sitting, he appeared tall enough that few would have called him short. Still, he was clearly expecting trouble.

Smart fellow.

Finn inclined his head as he stopped in front of the table. "I understand you seek information about Lady Belfort."

The fellow leaned back, bracing hands on the table as if to assure Finn he was unarmed. "I have information about Lady Belfort, thank you, kindly."

"I was not offering," Finn said. "Why are you here?"

Once more he looked Finn up and down. "No question why you're here. You're one of the Imperial Guards."

"I am," Finn admitted. "And you are?"

"Ever hear of a Bow Street Runner?"

He had. One had arrested Count Montalban, the prince's brother, on a trumped-up charge that had nearly seen him hanged. "Yes," Finn said. "He is an officer of the court."

"A member of the magistrate's office," he corrected him. "And we can be hired by anyone to look into possible criminal activity."

Criminal activity? Surely not Lady Belfort. "Who hired you now?" Finn demanded.

The Runner shrugged. "That I am not at liberty to say. Just know that important people are looking into your sweet lady friend."

The implication was insulting, to him and to the lady. "Lady Belfort is my patroness," Finn said. "Nothing more."

"She wasn't the lady to which I was referring. I may have been asking questions about Lady Belfort, but I was sent to learn more about your Miss Winchester."

Finn recoiled. "That cannot be."

His smile was satisfied, as if Finn had told him more than expected. "I assure you it is. What do you know about her?"

That she was kind and patient with children, that her smile made the world feel right and good. Her Grace the Duchess of Wey trusted her to care for her sons. Lady Belfort trusted her to share her home.

Were they all mad?

"What do *you* know about her?" Finn countered.

"She ran away from her last post as if she'd nicked the silver, only there's no word on anything being stolen," he supplied. "She claimed to have attended a seminary for young ladies, though the headmistress there refused to confirm it to me. She doesn't apparently like to talk about her family, but if there are any left, I'll find them."

She could not have appeared at the house party from nowhere. She had a past—a father who had committed a scandal, she'd said. But if there was more, he would not help the Runner uncover it.

For it didn't matter what she'd done. His king and prince had not been perfect, though Prince Otto Leopold had certainly tried. Finn had protected them. He was sworn to protect Abigail now.

"Word to the wise," the Runner said, as if he could see the thoughts churning through Finn's mind. "A gentleman like you ought to distance yourself. It's only a matter of time before I discover what she's hiding."

"Nothing," Finn promised him. "You work in vain. Miss Winchester is the finest lady I have had call to meet."

"Perhaps," he said. "But people don't generally go to the trouble of hiring a Runner to no purpose."

Finn inclined his head and left. His fists were balling at his sides. He shook them out. The Runner and whoever had hired him were wrong. Abigail couldn't be hiding anything.

But someone was.

It was easy for Abigail to pretend all was well with the world when she was at Rose Hill. Her room was just down the corridor from Meredith's, and she had no doubt it had housed many a titled guest. Decorated in French blue, white, and gold, it had dainty furnishings and soft chairs. Lady Belfort's own maid came in to help Abigail dress and undress, and she never seemed to mind in the least. The expectations on Abigail were minimal and pleasant, as if she were a guest instead of a companion. It was almost as if the entire scandal with her father had never happened.

The others whom Meredith was sponsoring were having more difficulty, alas. Only Mr. Roth had found a position thus far—as a guard at the steam works beyond Weyton, where he would start next week, and she tried not to feel guilty for being glad Finn could remain at her side. Unfortunately, Mr. Keller had been deemed too young by the headmaster of the boys' school to teach there.

Meredith had not been pleased. "I can generally tell who is suited to what position," she had told Abigail and Finn last night as they were eating an excellent dinner of roast venison in walnut sauce. "I have never had to place anyone twice."

From under the table came a mew, as if in protest. Finn raised his brows.

"Do not feed her," Meredith cautioned, forking up a mouthful of savory pudding. "You will only encourage her."

"How can you ignore such a plea?" Abigail asked, tilting her head to try to catch a glimpse of the cat.

"Especially when one's heart is kind," Finn said.

She straightened, face heating, to find him smiling at her from across the table.

"I will own that it is difficult," Meredith allowed. "That is how she ingratiated herself to me in the beginning, by mewling at me and gazing at me with those great eyes as I trudged home one night. I have never been able to resist a plea for help, from a starving kitten or a lost lady."

Her gaze pinned Abigail in her seat, and Finn's smile faded.

Lost? She had tried hard not to allow that adjective to describe her, in any sense. "I can only thank you again for your generosity," she said, mouth suddenly dry. She reached for her goblet.

"I'm delighted to have you with me," Meredith assured her. "Though, if you are expecting trouble, I would prefer to know so I could be prepared to counter it."

Abigail shook her head as she lowered the glass. "I am learning that trouble comes when one least expects it, your ladyship. I would not willingly bring it to your door. But I cannot foresee every possibility. Even the most astute banker can fail in that regard."

As she knew to her sorrow.

At least they had had plenty of visitors this morning to keep her and Meredith busy. The first had been the Rose Hill bailiff, a tall, gruff fellow who had sat with her ladyship in the library and explained the repairs needed around the estate because of the gale in August. Meredith had agreed to his proposal and sent him off. Abigail had kept Fortune entertained.

The second was a pair of elderly widows, who perched

on the withdrawing room chairs like contented ravens in their mourning black and talked of weather and crops and Sunday's sermon. Abigail sat and smiled and responded genially to any question put directly to her.

A shame Finn had left for the village. She might have shared a smile with him. Mr. Tanner had stationed himself downstairs near the front door. She had a feeling only a pretty lady might have coaxed him up to join them.

The next visitor was the Duchess of Wey herself. She and Meredith spent a good little while catching up on activities and acquaintances before Meredith held up a hand.

"You know I enjoy a good coz, Jane," she said, "but you are clearly bursting. You had a reason for visiting."

"Never could be the proper duchess," she said with a wink to Abigail. "Yes, I came with a purpose." She leaned forward, wrinkling the cerulean blue wool of her fashionable gown. "I must know. Have you heard from Julian?"

Meredith sighed. "No. I take it you've had no word from Larissa either?"

The duchess shook her dark head. "No, and I tell myself not to worry. The mail can be difficult coming from the Continent."

"Ships must rely on the tides and weather," Meredith acknowledged. "The mail must travel by courier at times, a farmer's wagon at others."

"And the sun must shine and the wind blow softly," she said with a smile. "All that combined, I would like to know my daughter and her husband are safe. I'm sure you feel the same about Julian."

"I do," Meredith said. "But we can do nothing except wait."

Abigail hurt for them. Waiting had never felt satisfying.

"Perhaps we should look at the notes the villagers

sent," she suggested to Meredith after the duchess had taken her leave.

"Excellent idea," Meredith said, as if determined to regain her usual purpose. They repaired to the library, and she handed Abigail a half dozen missives while she took a similar set.

Abigail raised her brows. "They were busy."

"Indeed." Meredith frowned at the first of hers. "This is a suggestion about the guard post at the steam works. Mr. Roth has already filled that."

Abigail glanced down at the top one on her lap, which had been written in a flowery hand with an excess of curls and flourishes. "Someone would like an escort for a lady of breeding and style. No name is specified." She lifted the thick piece of vellum and nearly sneezed at the heavy rose scent.

"Likely one of the ladies who was glancing our way at services," Meredith concluded, shuffling through her own. "Assistant linen draper—oh, I think not. Blacksmith apprentice—they *use* swords not craft them. Pig farmer!" She dropped the lot. "These won't do at all."

Abigail had similar luck with hers. "It looks as if you'll be writing more letters."

Meredith sighed. "Let us hope the next batch brings better results."

She was hard at it when Finn returned early afternoon. Abigail put a finger to her lips, then motioned him out of the library before he could take up his place along the wall.

"Meredith is trying to concentrate," she cautioned. "Let's go for a walk and give her a little peace."

He agreed, and she went to fetch her pelisse. Thank goodness she'd thought to save her favorite—a summer-sky blue with quilting down the front and a ruffle at her throat. But when she reached the entry hall, Finn was nowhere to be seen.

"Outside, Miss Winchester," the footman offered helpfully. He leaned closer. "He checked every shrub and tree along the drive."

Of course he would.

She found him waiting on the drive.

"Lady Belfort writes a great many letters," he mused as they set off from the house, down the lane she knew led to the cottage he shared with the other guards. The sun winked through wider gaps in the leaves, and the air was moist.

"She is trying to locate positions for you," Abigail reminded him. "She is also trying to reach her husband. She misses him terribly. I find it very romantic."

He grunted as if he had no opinion on the matter.

"Come now, Finn," she teased. "You've watched your prince and his brother court. And I know you to have the heart of a poet."

His gaze snapped to hers, and it was the first time she had seen him startled. "A poet?"

"I have not forgotten your impassioned description of your country, sir," she informed him, stopping beneath the spreading branches of a massive old oak, its leaves turning the same golden brown of his eyes. She placed her hand against his chest. "You said you heard the alpine winds blowing, here."

He gazed down at her, and all at once she was aware of how close she stood.

"Are you in trouble?" he asked.

Something colder than an alpine wind blew through her. Had she said something? Done something? Or had someone else here recognized her and filled his ears with poison?

"No," she said in her best governess' voice, hand falling. "I have done nothing wrong."

He nodded. "Very well."

That was it? He was willing to accept her word? How very refreshing!

"Thank you," she said. "I suppose we all have things in our past we would prefer to forget."

He stepped back. "Some more than others."

She found it hard to believe he could ever be anything less than honorable. It seemed to be embedded in his skin. But after his kind acceptance, she could hardly question him. Besides, she had known her father's scandal would require her to keep him at arm's length.

Why did she suddenly long to pull him close?

CHAPTER SEVEN

ON WEDNESDAY, ABIGAIL was in the library with Meredith, who was composing a letter to her husband, even though Abigail knew she feared it might never reach him. Abigail was ostensibly reading. She had a book, and it was open in her lap. She even turned a page on occasion. But she kept glancing at Finn, who was standing near the window. The sun had peeked out of hiding, and the light turned his eyes to gold. Even when she attempted to read, she felt his gaze lingering on her.

Fortune kept ambling between the two of them as if she were carrying love notes. Abigail was almost annoyed when Mr. Cowls appeared in the doorway.

"Miss Hewett and Mrs. Daring are desirous of renewing your acquaintance, your ladyship," he intoned.

Neither name meant anything to Abigail, but she caught herself tensing nonetheless. She had never been privy to the list of those who had invested in the Poyais scheme, only the list of those who had dared journey forth and never returned.

"I had no idea Julia was back from Bath." Meredith set down her quill. "By all means, Mr. Cowls, show her and Mrs. Daring to the withdrawing room. We will join them shortly."

"Very good, your ladyship."

As he left them, Meredith rose, her lavender skirts swinging. She seemed attached to the color, which closely matched her eyes, for Abigail had yet to see her wear any other. Today it was a charming wool gown with a white tucker that had a high, ruffled collar.

"These people are well known to you?" Finn asked, pushing off from the wall to accompany them toward the door.

"Very well known," Meredith assured him. "Julia's parents moved into the area when she was a girl, but she grew up here." She glanced at Abigail. "I think you will enjoy her company. She is about your age, has her own opinions, and is not overly demur about sharing them."

Someone her age, who had lived all her life in Surrey, would surely be safe. "I look forward to meeting her," Abigail said.

Finn must have felt equally comfortable, for he allowed Meredith and Abigail to precede him through the door into the withdrawing room. He then took up a position in the corner, where he could see through the door and the wide windows overlooking the garden. Surely he didn't think anyone would scale the wall in broad daylight to accost them!

Miss Hewett cast him a quick, curious glance before turning her attention to Meredith. She had fiery red hair carefully confined under a jaunty straw hat and brown eyes that sparkled, as if she were planning mischief. Abigail wasn't surprised when Fortune promptly hopped up onto her fashionable spruce-colored skirts and made herself at home.

"Lady Belfort!" she declared, "and dear Fortune! How delightful to have you with us again."

"And how delightful to see you," Meredith assured her, "and you as well, Mrs. Daring.

The young lady's companion was small and thin, with flyaway white hair that was already coming free of its pins and puckered blue eyes that tended to blink. Her tiny hands fluttered in front of her grey pelisse, as if she wasn't sure whether to take it off or hug it close in protection.

"You are too kind," Mrs. Daring said. A lace-edged handkerchief appeared in her hand, and she dabbed at her eyes as if quite overcome by the recognition.

"Allow me to make you known to my companions," Meredith said. "This is Abigail Winchester, who has graciously agreed to keep me company while my Julian is traveling. And the gentleman glowering from the corner is Mr. Finn Huber, of the Batavarian Imperial Guard."

Miss Hewett had smiled at Abigail, her gloved hand stroking Fortune's fur, but at the mention of the Imperial Guard, her hand froze. "The Imperial Guards? I thought they had all decamped for home."

"All except four," Meredith clarified, taking her seat. Abigail sat nearby, making sure she could see Finn. "I will be finding them positions, as they wish to stay in England."

Miss Hewett's smile was strained. "Which four?"

"Mr. Roth, Mr. Huber, Mr. Keller, and Mr. Tanner," Abigail supplied.

"You were at the ball the Duchess of Wey gave this summer," Meredith added. "You may recall meeting Mr. Roth, Mr. Huber, and Mr. Keller. Mr. Tanner was at the house party as well, though he was on assignment for the prince and spent most of his time moving about the island, watching for any danger. I am merely thankful that worry has passed."

"And do they all attend you?" Miss Hewett asked with a glance to the door, as if she thought to spy a black, gilt-encrusted uniform any moment.

Oh, not another one! Were all the ladies in the area smitten?

"Every morning at the very least," Meredith explained. "And I believe Mr. Keller is due to spell Mr. Huber this evening after dinner."

"Tanner tonight," Finn corrected her.

Fortune twitched in Miss Hewett's lap, and she hurriedly began petting her again. "How interesting. I'm sure you'll secure them all positions, and they will be leaving shortly."

"I had hoped within the fortnight," Meredith said. "I don't suppose you are in need of a bodyguard, Julia."

"That would be lovely," Mrs. Daring said with a deep sigh. "I can only do so much."

Abigail struggled to imagine she could do anything at all.

Miss Hewett cast her companion a fond glance before answering Meredith. "My father hovers enough as it is. Daring is sufficient for my needs."

Mrs. Daring sighed again.

Miss Hewett pulled back her hand and started to rise, sending Fortune leaping for the floor. "We should not keep you overly long. I merely wanted to see you for myself. Perhaps you'll have more time to visit when the fortnight is over and your guards are gone."

Abigail frowned. London calls often didn't last more than a quarter hour, but Miss Hewett and her companion must have taken some trouble to reach them, and she was friends with Meredith. Why leave so soon?

"We will see each other before the fortnight ends," Meredith said, rising as well. "I expect you will be at the assembly a week from Friday."

Miss Hewett waved a hand. "Oh, the assemblies are all so dull. Likely I will remain at home."

"But you told me expressly how much you were looking forward to it," Mrs. Daring said, managing to gain her feet and tottering as she did so. "Did we not have a new ballgown made for the purpose?"

"You must be thinking of another ball," Miss Hewett assured her. She turned to Abigail with a ready smile. "It was a pleasure to meet you, Miss Winchester. I do hope we may become better acquainted in the future." She sailed from the room, her companion trailing behind like an anchor loosed from its mooring.

"I will make sure they leave," Finn said, striding after them.

Abigail exchanged glances with Meredith. "Is she always so flighty?"

"Never," Meredith said with a frown. "She seems to have taken exception to the Imperial Guards. I wonder why."

It rained Wednesday night, leaving the trees dark and the sky clean on Thursday morning as Finn, Keller, and Roth made their way to the main house. Finn breathed in the air, closing his eyes a moment to savor the scents—wet wood, earth, smoke. It almost smelled like home.

Roth and Keller were both studying the woods as if expecting trouble. He had told them and Tanner about his meeting with the Bow Street Runner, although he had not mentioned the matter to Lady Belfort and Abigail. He and the others were a match for the fellow, and there was still much they did not know.

"This becomes tedious," Roth said, black boots thudding against the lane as if they were as heavy as his thoughts. "Every interview seems designed to show us how ill-equipped we are to be anything but soldiers."

"We could join a British regiment," Keller suggested. "Though I am cheered by the fact that we have better accommodations than many we've shared, and we have food and friends a-plenty."

Roth nodded, but his scowl said he was struggling.

Finn understood. They were used to being on duty from breakfast to dinner or dinner to breakfast, patrolling the palace, standing guard at state functions, and escorting their king, his sons, and his courtiers about for protection.

Leisure moments had been spent drilling or tending to their equipment. There had been no such thing as a half-day off much less days of lolling about, waiting. Even with Roth's imposed drills, the time stretched.

And why wait? Finn had yet to be sent for an interview, though he could not mind overmuch with the Bow Street Runner nosing around. Roth was working, but he returned to the house in the early morning hours, tight-lipped, and eventually fell into bed to sleep most of the day. Was this their future? Where was the honor, the glory? The purpose?

The door opened to Roth's rap, as usual, but a grey shadow flashed past his boots.

"Stop her!" Mr. Cowls' voice was surprisingly sharp. "Do not let her escape."

Keller reacted first, diving for the fleeing cat, but Fortune slipped through his fingers and dashed for the pond.

Finn turned to keep her in sight. "There, under those bushes."

"Not for long," Roth declared, striding in that direction.

Fortune burst from the greenery to frisk down the path, as if taunting them.

"Did you catch her?" Abigail appeared in the doorway, face flushed.

Finn shook his head even as Keller followed Roth down the path. "She was too quick."

Her hands worried before her daisy-embroidered gown. "It's my fault. I didn't see her leave the withdrawing room. I should have been watching. Will you help me find her?"

"Of course," Finn said, and they set out after his comrades.

The flagstone path opposite the door wound through tree and shrub, many ragged now with the promise of winter. Up ahead, Keller called Fortune's name. The trees nearest them rustled.

Finn stopped, glanced up, thinking to spy two copper-colored eyes gazing down at him. Instead, two narrow blue eyes that might have been called squinty stared down from a wrinkled face. Finn put Abigail behind him.

"Who are you?" he demanded. "What are you doing here?"

In answer, the fellow dropped to the ground on the other side of the tree and took off running, small frame weaving through the bushes with ease.

Finn pivoted and braced his hands on Abigail's shoulders. "Return to the house. Now. Tell Tanner to lock the doors."

Abigail stood, rooted in place. She'd only seen the man who had warned her in London for a moment, but she could not doubt the fellow in the tree was the same person. He had followed her, then.

No time to understand what he hoped to gain by it. Finn had his duty, and she had hers.

"Follow him," she countered. "I will find Fortune."

He hesitated a moment, then snapped a nod and darted off after the fellow.

Stomach knotting at the thought of the trouble she had brought on him and Meredith, she hurried forward, gaze sweeping over the bushes. "Fortune! Fortune! Please, darling, come to me!"

Mr. Keller strode around a tree, and Abigail nearly sagged in relief at the sight of the grey-coated cat up in his arms. The delicate growl and narrowed eyes proclaimed Fortune's displeasure.

"I caught her by the pond," Mr. Keller said. He stretched out his arms toward Abigail as if to offer her the cat.

Fortune dug in her claws, and he winced. She turned her head away from Abigail and regarded him fixedly, as if accusing him of the darkest crime.

"Perhaps I should carry her inside," he suggested. "Would you call in Roth and Huber?"

"I'll find Mr. Roth," she said, "but Mr. Huber has gone in pursuit of a stranger we discovered watching the house."

His eyes widened. "Then I should be the one finding Roth." He unhooked Fortune's claws from his sleeve and managed to transfer the cat to Abigail's arms. "Go, quickly. We will protect you."

Abigail nodded and hurried toward the house.

In her arms, Fortune hissed, fur as prickly as a porcupine.

Abigail loosened her hold just enough to keep the cat from escaping again. "I'm so sorry. This will only take a moment."

As she came out onto the drive, the sun dove behind a cloud, casting the area into shadow. She fought a shiver. Fortune wasn't the only one feeling uncomfortable. Had the man in the tree come because of Poyais? Was she never to be free of it?

"Abigail?"

She jumped, then hugged Fortune closer as Finn stepped out of the shadows, Mr. Roth and Mr. Keller right behind.

"Gentlemen," she greeted, hoping her voice didn't sound as breathless as she feared. "What news of our unexpected visitor?"

"He had a horse waiting along the road," Mr. Roth reported. "We could not catch him."

Finn glanced back the way they had come. "We must speak with Lady Belfort."

She nodded, and they set out for the house.

"Are you all right?" Finn asked beside her.

She would have to find a way to explain to him and

Meredith. For now, she focused on her minor success. "Fine. Just glad Fortune is safe." Hand stroking the soft fur, she glanced his way. His dark brows were knit, his shoulders tight. She could not help but think herself at least partially to blame.

"He was here for me," she said.

Finn's frown only deepened, but Mr. Roth pinned her with a look.

"Why?" he demanded.

Any answer she might give would only cause more questions. "I'll explain what I know to you and to Meredith," she promised before chivying them all into the house.

They found Meredith just coming down the stairs, with Mr. Tanner at her heels, having been alerted to the cat's escape. She readily took Fortune, alternating between scolding her and crooning endearments as they all returned to the withdrawing room. Fortune suffered the demonstration while glowering at Mr. Keller as he took a seat across from them. Mr. Tanner leaned against the hearth. Finn and Mr. Roth saluted Meredith before taking seats as well.

"Is she all right?" Abigail asked, bending closer to the cat.

Fortune raised her head to bump against Abigail's fingers, the touch somehow encouraging.

"Fine," Meredith assured her. "Most likely my nerves are more torn than hers. Why does she insist on trying to escape?"

"Perhaps there is more to interest her outside," Mr. Tanner suggested.

"More to interest us as well," Finn put in, leaning forward. "There was a man, Lady Belfort, up in a tree, watching the house."

She froze, fingers in her pet's fur. "What? When?"

"When we came out to find Fortune," Abigail explained, sinking onto the sofa next to them. "And I recognized him. Before I left London, he confronted me and warned me to keep silent. I don't know why, but today, he was studying the house."

"He may have been the one the postmaster mentioned," Finn said. "He fit the description. And there is more you should know. When I went into the village the other day, I talked with a Bow Street Runner, sent to ask questions."

Meredith raised her chin. "And you waited to tell me until now?"

Abigail could only agree. As if he knew he had disappointed them, he lowered his gaze. "He was not here about you, your ladyship. He came seeking Miss Winchester."

Abigail's heart jerked, and she pressed a hand to her chest. "Me? Why?"

"That, he would not say," Finn replied. "But I am assured it is a mistake. You committed no crime."

Meredith turned her lavender gaze Abigail's way, as if wondering.

Abigail refused to flinch. "That is only too true. None of what happened to me was of my making, except these utterly unsuitable gowns!"

They were all staring at her now, and she forced in a breath. *Composure.* Oh, why was it so elusive at times?

"Perhaps," Meredith said gently, "you should explain."

Abigail swallowed. She had only spoken the truth. Yet would they see it that way? Would they too try to hold her accountable for her father's mistakes?

She glanced from Meredith, who was studying her with head cocked, to Mr. Tanner and Mr. Keller, who were leaning forward expectantly, to Mr. Roth, whose arms were crossed over his chest as if he awaited some dire confession.

Finn nodded to her, golden eyes warm and trusting.

She drew in a breath. "Have you heard of the Poyais scandal?"

"Certainly," Meredith said. "It dominated the papers for months. Indeed, it was so audacious I am stunned how many were taken in by it."

Roth dropped his arms. "What is this scandal? I have never heard of Poyais."

"No one had," Abigail told him. "And it turns out it never existed."

CHAPTER EIGHT

Abigail could only be glad when Meredith spoke up. She was finding it difficult enough to explain the scheme.

"An officer who had distinguished himself in the war with Napoleon traveled to Bolivia some years ago in search of adventure," Meredith elaborated. "He apparently distinguished himself there as well. The British press ever sang his praises. So, when Colonel MacGregor returned, claiming to have been granted his own kingdom along the Caribbean Sea, many were ready to believe it."

"He didn't just claim he had land," Abigail said, determined that they should understand. "He claimed he had built a city with wide streets and lovely homes. He talked of rich farms and hills full of gold, silver, and precious gems, all there for the taking by anyone with a little ambition. He convinced dozens to invest, hundreds to migrate, promising positions, homes, and places at court. He was received by the Court of St. James!"

"Your king was taken in?" Finn asked, brow puckered.

"Everyone was taken in," Abigail assured him.

"Colonel MacGregor is a true blackguard," Meredith agreed. "Those settlers who sailed to populate his utopia found only thick jungles and disease."

Her throat was tight, her eyes burning. "Disease and so much more. The ships that carried them were blown out to sea in a terrible storm. Their supplies dwindled.

They were eventually rescued by the British colony at Honduras, but by then only a handful remained."

Fortune pulled from Meredith's grip to slip onto Abigail's lap and cuddle close. She ran her hand down the fur.

"There is no scandal in being deceived," Finn said. "The wrong lies with the deceiver."

She heard his comrades murmuring agreement.

"There is more," Abigail said, lifting her gaze from the grey-coated cat. "Colonel MacGregor approached several banks, seeking loans to fund the transport of so many people and mine the vast wealth. My father convinced the bank he managed to issue such a loan. For his championship of the cause, the colonel granted him the post of Royal Banker to Poyais."

"What cruelty," Meredith murmured.

"My father resigned his post and sailed with the first group of settlers. My mother and I sold all we had, including any clothes unsuitable for a tropical climate, and waited for him to send for us. It was nearly a year before the news came, a year of increasingly frantic letters that went nowhere. You see, Poyais was a myth. My father had died on that sunny shore he thought would be his making."

"Oh, Abigail," Meredith said.

She could not stop for the kindness or she would never finish. "No one wished to associate with the family of the man who had aided Colonel MacGregor in his predations. My mother and I lived on her dower settlement, and she gave music lessons, but she died of a broken heart about six months later. And I entered service to escape those who wanted to see me suffer for my father's mistake. Unfortunately that has not gone well."

"You are an excellent governess," Finn said, as if challenging anyone to disagree.

"I certainly tried," Abigail said. "It was temporary positions at first—filling in for other governesses who were ill or helping at events like the Duchess of Wey's house party. My first permanent assignment was with Lord Granbury, but I had only been serving him a short time before he told me he knew enough to ruin me and demanded that I prove my loyalty to him."

She could not help the shudder at the memory of how he'd stood over her, hand on her shoulder, as if he thought to possess her.

Finn was bristling, but Meredith shook her head.

"I was under the impression Lord Granbury thought rather highly of you," she said with a frown.

Under Abigail's hand, Fortune shifted, as if she was of the same opinion.

"He did not mention Poyais specifically," Abigail acknowledged, "but the implication was clear. He was only the last in a long line to judge me or think they could take advantage of my misfortune."

"Curs," Meredith snapped. "The lot of them. It was hardly your fault your father was misled."

"They needed someone to blame," Roth said. "It is a common, if disreputable, failing."

"You have no reason to hide," Finn said. "You did not cause this."

She sucked in a breath, holding his words closer than the cat. "I know. But sometimes, I wonder whether I should have questioned him, questioned the colonel. It all seemed so wonderful. Perhaps I should have suspected it couldn't be true."

"You and dozens of others must be asking the same questions," Meredith said. "But I quite agree with Mr. Roth. It is easy to excuse our own lapses by blaming them on others. We will not make the same mistake."

They all nodded.

Abigail's gaze sought Finn's. His face had softened, and he rubbed his hands along his thighs, as if he wished he could reach out and gather her to him in comfort.

"Is that why the Bow Street Runner and spy trouble us, then?" Keller asked, glancing around. "Someone wants to punish Miss Winchester for what this colonel did?"

"I don't know," Abigail admitted. "But I fear as much."

"I cannot like it," Roth said. "With your permission, your ladyship, I will speak to Mr. Cowls about security, and I will ride the perimeter."

Meredith inclined her head. "Thank you, Mr. Roth. That would help set my mind at ease."

He rose, bowed, and strode out.

Meredith sighed, then put on her usual calm demeanor like a new gown. It seemed Abigail wasn't the only one to rely on composure in a tight spot.

"I had hoped we might discuss next steps this morning," she said, "but I find myself in a difficult position. Mr. Huber, I wrote to the Marquess of Kendall concerning a position that might be open on his estate. Villa Romanesque, as his house is called, is about an hour to the south of us. He and his wife Ivy are old friends. However, I would not want to lose you if we have need of you here."

"Nor would I feel comfortable leaving, your ladyship," he said, though his gaze veered to Abigail.

Meredith looked to Keller. "There is a position open at the Garvey estate. Do you have any experience with keeping game?"

Keller's usually rosy cheeks paled. "No, your ladyship. I was born and raised in the capitol city. Mr. Huber knows more about animals than I do."

"My parents raised dairy cows," Finn explained. "I have had to deal with bear and wolf, but it was many years ago, and I doubt that qualifies as experience to be a gamekeeper."

"Likely not," Meredith said. "Pity. You'd do better as a bailiff. As for you, Mr. Tanner," she shot a look to the third guardsman, "I received word from your last interview. It seems you were too flippant for your potential employer's tastes."

He pressed a hand to the chest of his satin-striped waistcoat. "Flippant? Me?"

Meredith cocked a dark brow.

Abigail could not doubt the report. The chestnut-haired guardsman saw entirely too much humor in the world. Finn was far steadier, even-tempered. Her rock.

"Regardless," Meredith said, "I will endeavor to find you a position more in keeping with your character."

"Rider in Astley's Amphitheater, perhaps?" he suggested, light in his brown eyes. "Bodyguard to some famous explorer ready to take a round-the-world tour?"

"Perhaps," she allowed. "I certainly did not foresee such difficulties when I agreed to sponsor you. I would have thought your training and experiences with His Royal Highness sufficient. But there seem to be some key aspects in which you require tutoring."

Abigail blinked. Tutoring? And here she was, a governess. Finally, a way to be of use.

"Perhaps," she said, "I could help teach you the ways of an English gentleman."

Standing along the wall to protect his king and prince, Finn had heard any number of conversations that shocked him. When another farm had been buried in an avalanche, and he had been powerless to help. When the minister for the king of Italy had regretfully informed King Frederick that his presence was no longer wanted as an exile in that country. When Giselle's father had berated the head of the Imperial Guard for promoting an upstart like Finn to service.

Abigail's story was worse. He felt the wrongness of it in the marrow of his bones, painful. She was innocent of any crime, yet she was being made to pay the price for her father's mistake. It wasn't right, and he could do nothing to make it so.

All he could do was protect. And all she could do, it seemed, was teach.

"What an excellent suggestion," Lady Belfort said. "A little brushing up on etiquette might help them better show to advantage in interviews. You can start this very afternoon, when Mr. Roth returns from his patrol."

Keller exchanged glances with Finn. "But we must drill, your ladyship," he protested. "Mr. Roth is insistent that we keep our skills fresh. We were planning on swords this afternoon."

"More importantly," Finn said, "we must discover the nature of our enemy: who sent the spy and why."

"A wise course," she agreed. "We will alert the village to watch for strangers and bring any news to us. Mr. Cowls has an amazing facility for learning about local happenings. In the meantime, we will remain vigilant, as Mr. Roth suggested. Mr. Tanner and Mr. Keller?"

The two snapped to attention.

"It might be best if you stayed close to the house for now. Go see if the garden would be a suitable place for your drills. I will send Finn down shortly to join you."

They saluted her and turned to go. Tanner raised his brows at Finn again as he passed.

"Your ladyship?" Finn asked in the quiet that followed.

Lady Belfort stood and shook out her skirts. "I merely want you to keep Abigail company. I must speak to Mr. Cowls, and I would prefer Fortune not be so close to the door, given her recent escapade. Abigail will watch Fortune, and you will watch Abigail."

Finn frowned as she passed him, until he caught a twitch in her eye. Had she just winked at him?

"She's giving us a moment," Abigail said, fingers stroking the cat in her lap.

Fortune pulled away, dropped to the carpet, and went to the window, as if offering them privacy as well.

"Why?" Finn asked, venturing closer.

"You have been assigned to guard me," she said, "and you now know my darkest secret. Have I given you a disgust of me?"

"Never."

The word must have come out more forcefully than he intended, for her eyes widened.

"I agree with Lady Belfort," he said, gentling his voice. "You are not to be blamed for what others have done."

"I can't help thinking I should have known," she argued. "Father was naturally reticent about discussing his work. It was a matter of pride as much as privacy for his clients. Yet when he told us he had accepted the position of banker for the Cazique of Poyais, I should have questioned him. And Mother kept joking I would be a princess." She bowed her head and drew in a breath.

Finn abandoned his position and went to kneel in front of her. Her head came up. The blue eyes searched his face as if seeking forgiveness, hope.

He took her hands in his. "You are not to blame," he repeated. "Any more than I am to blame for not reaching my parents and little sister when the avalanche struck. I was in the barn with the cows when I heard the rumble. We were trapped for days until neighbors dug us out. Sometimes, the world conspires against us like that. Sometimes, we can only endure."

She nodded. "I think that way too. Father passed, Mother passed, friends turned away. Preston Netherfield, the man I had thought to wed, was forced to abandon me to preserve his reputation for his family's sake."

Preston Netherfield, her devoted suitor. She'd probably had dozens. The daughter of a well-placed banker, possessed of such beauty and poise, would not want for attention. Yet he could not help thinking the man a villain and a fool for leaving her side when she'd needed him most.

"And you went on with your life," he encouraged her.

"I did. I try to tell myself it's perfectly acceptable to survive, even if others didn't."

Her breath caught, and he pressed her hands. "Then survive. Thrive. Make something of your life that pleases you."

Her gaze brushed his again. "Is that what you're doing here in England? Making a life that pleases you?"

He sighed. "I am no longer certain what pleases me other than to be of use to someone."

"But you *were* of use to someone. I know your prince valued your service. Others will as well. I certainly appreciate it. When you are near, Finn, I feel as if everything will come out right, and I haven't felt that way in a long time."

She knew the words that fed him. He wanted to spoon them in and savor the taste. "Then I am honored to be of service." He gave her hands another squeeze and rose. "Now, how do you intend to spend the afternoon before dinner?"

"Why?" she asked, head tilted to meet his gaze.

"Because I need to know which wall to stand along."

Abigail felt as if she were a rug, taken out, shaken, beaten, and inspected for fleas. But at least there were no more secrets to hide. Finn, Meredith, and the others knew the whole of it.

Meredith did not appear to agree. She returned quickly

and ordered Finn down to the garden with the others. He went reluctantly, glancing twice at Abigail on the way out. Meredith shut the door. "We must talk."

Abigail's spirits sank like a log half-burned by the fire. "Very well. But allow me first to apologize. We talked so much about my past that I forgot entirely why we all ventured outside in the first place. Fortune escaped. I should have noticed when she left me and warned Mr. Cowls to keep her from the door."

Meredith waved a hand. "When Fortune wishes to go somewhere, few can gainsay her." She glanced to where her pet was now perched on the wide windowsill, tail swinging, as she watched the goings on in the garden below. "Though I cannot help but wonder whether she was trying to draw our attention to the stranger."

Given the cat's legendary insights, it was quite possible. Her vantage point out one of the windows might have allowed her to spot the fellow before the rest of them.

Meredith smoothed down her lavender skirts and returned her gaze to Abigail. "I must apologize as well. The reason I was surprised that Lord Granbury disliked you is that I asked Sir Matthew to look into who might have been following you in London. He and Lady Bateman enjoy looking into little mysteries."

Abigail stiffened on the chair. "You had me investigated?"

"No," Meredith said. "I had your enemies investigated. Sir Matthew interviewed Lord Granbury, who was highly complimentary and offered to hire you back at an increase in wages."

"I don't understand," Abigail said with a frown. "Lord Granbury made it sound as if he thought me a fallen woman, and one that could be easily persuaded. He must have realized by now that neither would be a good influence on his daughters."

"Very odd," Meredith agreed. "And yet we have another oddity as well. Apparently, a gentleman came seeking you at your lodging house after you'd gone. Who might that have been?"

Abigail shook her head, feeling as if she had set out to sea without a compass. "I have no idea. I told no one, not even the employment agency, where I was staying. Could it have been this fellow today?"

"Doubtful," Meredith said, studying her. "I understand he was too common to describe. That would not match our spy." She cocked her head. "No suitors hoping to make their case? A brother determined to protect you?"

Preston came to mind, but he had severed all acquaintance weeks before she had become a governess. She still teared up remembering how he'd railed against the fate that had separated them. But he was the sole support for his mother and two younger sisters. He had to protect his reputation so he could continue providing for them.

"I have only myself to protect me," she said. "And now Finn, because you requested it of him."

She tsked. "I have a feeling he would have volunteered had I not asked him. But I understand. I felt the same way once. Relying on any gentleman seemed unwise."

Abigail stared at her. "What changed your mind?"

"My Julian," she said with a smile. "You heard Mr. Summers, the postmaster, the other day, I suppose. I was once Mary Rose, of Rose Hill, and Julian's parents had a home in the area. We grew up together. We pledged ourselves to marry when we were quite young, but, like you, I lost everything on my mother's death. And Julian did not ride to my rescue. It wasn't until later that I realized a cruel family member was preventing my letters asking for help from reaching him. I thought he had abandoned me."

The story was too much like her own. "How did you ever find a way back to each other?"

"I will admit to some anger and bitterness over the

matter," she allowed. "But when we met again, it soon became clear that he thought me equally as hard-hearted. You see, the same wicked family member had conspired to keep Julian's letters from me. Once we realized the fact, we were able to learn to trust each other again."

She might have wished for such good fortune with Preston, but whatever feelings she'd had for him felt more like ash, cold and scattering in the wind. And she could not afford the other feelings that were growing.

Fortune jumped down from the window and wandered over to pin Meredith with a look.

"Misbehaving, are they?" she asked the cat. Then she glanced up at Abigail. "Perhaps you should go see what mischief Finn and the others have started now."

CHAPTER NINE

ABIGAIL HEARD THE clash of metal before she saw the combatants. They must have found the rear garden suitable, for Tanner and Finn had faced off on one of the rows, coats draped over bushes and swords in hand. She had never seen a gentleman practice fencing, but she couldn't immediately spot anything that looked amiss.

Indeed, it was fascinating. The swords had a slight curve to one edge—cutlasses, she seemed to remember them being called. Finn and Tanner stood about five feet apart. Finn appeared to be the attacker. Tanner only blocked. The cutlass flashed as Finn brought it down from the right, left, overhead, forward. It was as if he were reciting poetry, meter and rhythm mixing. With every lithe stroke, every powerful lunge, light and shadow played off well-trained muscle. She could not look away.

"Switch," Keller barked from one side, and Finn took up the defense, parrying each of Tanner's blows. The latter spied her first and pulled up his blade to salute her with it. "Miss Winchester."

"Nice try," Finn told him, his back to her. "You will not get under my guard so easily."

"He isn't lying," Abigail said, and Finn spun to face her.

Tanner smacked the flat of his blade against Finn's shoulder. Again, he spun, blade once more up.

"Roth would have your head for turning your back on an opponent," Keller told him with a grin.

"And I should have Tanner's for that maneuver," Finn countered.

"Gentlemen, please," Abigail said before things could grow any more heated. "Fortune seemed to think there was something of concern out here, so Lady Belfort sent me to check on you."

"Everything is fine," Finn said, pivoting to keep both her and Tanner in sight, blade at the ready.

Tanner flipped the sword to hold the hilt out to Abigail. "Care to try, Miss Winchester?"

Keller's grin widened.

She should demur, but she had to own to some curiosity. Gentlemen had once relied upon swords to protect themselves. She could not imagine carrying one about London or even Surrey. Clearly Finn was good at it. Perhaps she should give it a try.

She moved forward, and Tanner carefully transferred the hilt into her hand. The weight tugged at her arm, and she brought up her other hand to steady it.

"Very good," he said, coming in behind her. His arms wrapped around her as he guided her. "Keep it level. The smallest movement can deflect an opponent."

By the narrowing of Finn's eyes, he didn't like his friend quite so close to her. Neither did she. She shoved her elbow back and into his gut. "Like that?"

"Oomph." Tanner dropped his hold and staggered back. "Yes, quite like that."

Finn's smile tilted up. Keller choked back a laugh.

Both hands on the hilt, she moved the sword back and forth as she had seen them do. It was like trying to slice through fabric with a knife. "I don't see how you could fight very long with this. It's heavy."

"Tip up the blade, like this," Finn said, suiting word to action, and she raised the point higher. Immediately, she felt the difference.

"It's balanced, isn't it," she marveled.

"Well balanced," he assured her. "Strike it against mine."

Careful not to do anything that might harm him, she swung the blade. The clang reverberated up her arms.

"I don't think I like that," she said, lowering the blade. "I salute you both for your skill."

"Keller is the best," he said, even as Tanner came around her to retrieve the blade, careful, she noticed, to remain out of reach of her elbow.

"Middling," Keller said, wiggling one hand back and forth. "But Tanner learned a few tricks about boxing from Sir Matthew before we finished guarding Lady Moselle."

"You knew her as Miss Bateman," Finn explained. "She is now Lady Ashforde."

Odd that she and Lady Ashforde had both had a guard. But then again, perhaps neither of them had required one. "How fortunate for her," Abigail said.

Tanner edged closer. "I would be happy to show you how to defend yourself, Miss Winchester."

"She has no need to defend herself," Keller scolded him. "She has Huber at her side."

Even though he only meant as her bodyguard, her cheeks warmed.

Finn shook his head. "Did the king and prince know nothing about sword or fist? No, they excelled so that, should one of us fail, they could protect themselves."

"And their country," Tanner agreed. He looked to Abigail again and held up his fists. "So, what do you say, Miss Winchester? Care to know how to lay a fellow low?"

Abigail frowned. "Is it truly that easy?"

"No," Finn said, stepping in front of his colleague. "And if anyone is going to teach you, it will be me."

Tanner started chuckling, but he held up both hands, palm out, when Finn glared at him. "I surrender. I only hope you don't have to do the same."

Still laughing, he moved to join Keller at the side.

Finn could see himself reflected in Abigail's wide blue eyes. He had shocked her, but at least she was willing to try.

"It is not Sir Matthew's style you must copy," he explained. "Lady Ashforde learned from her brother, but she had to modify the forms to suit a lady."

"A shame she isn't here," Tanner quipped.

Finn ignored him. "So long as I am near, if you are threatened, you need only cry out. I will be there. Keep crying out so I can better locate you."

She nodded jerkily. Was he frightening her? That had not been his intent, but she needed to know what to do to keep herself safe. At some point, by circumstance or necessity, he would have to leave her side.

"If I am not near," he continued, "and someone approaches you from the front with ill purpose, thrust your arm out like this." He shoved his palm up and out. "Hard. Under his chin. Then run."

She lifted her skirts away from her leather slippers. "It's not easy to run in skirts, I fear."

"And that is the key word. Fear. It can be your helper. Lift your skirts and dash away as fast as you can to somewhere you can be safe. And scream."

Her smile broke free. "Apparently the important word is scream, not fear."

"It is a useful tool," Finn allowed.

Tanner could not stay out of the matter. He strode forward and wrapped his arms about Abigail, pinning her in place. "And what if someone should seize her from behind, like this?"

To Finn's surprise, Abigail snapped back her head,

catching Tanner on the chin. He stumbled away, arms dropping, and she dashed to Finn's side.

"Very good," Finn said as Tanner gained his balance and rubbed his chin.

"But not perfect," she said. "I forgot to scream."

Keller held up a hand before she could make good on the mischief shining in her eyes. "Please, do not. Roth will think something terrible has happened."

As it was, their leader did not return until nearly dinner, having crossed every inch of the estate, it seemed. He had found nothing untoward. Mr. Cowls had alerted Weyton, but the villagers reported no further sightings of strangers, not even the Bow Street Runner. The elderly butler looked almost apologetic that he could find nothing more. Indeed, if Finn hadn't chased the spy out to his horse and spoken to the Runner directly, he might have thought he'd imagined both of them.

Someone powerful, according to the Runner, wanted to know where Abigail was and what she was up to. He may have sent the spy.

So, Finn doubled his vigilance as he kept watch over Lady Belfort and Abigail. If they were outdoors, he walked the periphery, looking for any movements among the trees and shrubs. He rode up with the coachman, Mr. Haver, when they drove out. If they were inside the house, he moved from door to window and back several times an hour. Often, Fortune followed him, as if being just as vigilant. Lady Belfort raised a brow or shook her head, but Abigail watched him with concern in her pretty eyes.

At Roth's order, Keller and Tanner patrolled the estate three times a day and lengthened their drills with cutlass and fist, as if he expected a war to start any moment. But, over the next two days, no one spotted anything out of the ordinary.

How was he to keep Abigail safe when he did not know what was coming for her?

Meredith sighed on Saturday as she thumbed through the letters that had arrived in the post. Still no sign of that beloved hand. Was he safe? Did he miss her as much as she missed him? She had never thought she'd be one of those ladies who hung on the word of a gentleman, but she had to own she would have given much to see Julian walk through the door, red-gold hair glinting, smile warm.

Instead, a dark-haired guardsman strode from the window to the door, checking, always checking.

"Finn," she said, and he pulled up short, even as Abigail looked up from the book she had been reading. "Sit down."

He frowned. "Your ladyship?"

"Sit down," she repeated. "And if you cannot manage that, go downstairs and ask Cook when she expects to serve dinner this evening."

She was treating him like a servant, but he merely inclined his head and stalked from the room, Fortune following devotedly at his heels.

"Still no word from your husband in the post?" Abigail asked.

She had identified the problem precisely. "No," Meredith said with another sigh. "But I should not have taken it out on Finn."

"The mail is often delayed from the Continent," she offered. "You and Her Grace the Duchess of Wey were commenting on that earlier this week."

"So we were. I wish I could find your calm about the matter."

"It isn't my husband that's missing," she pointed out.

"Yet why do I sense you would be as calm had it been so?"

She closed the book and ran a hand over the leather cover. "When all these troubles beset us, I promised my mother I would remain composed. She certainly didn't need someone panicking at her side. After she died, I relied on composure to secure a position as a governess and to perform those duties. I find composure an easy refuge now."

"While I find composure entirely too highly valued at the moment," Meredith said, tossing the last of the letters on the pile in front of her. "Give me determination, conviction, passion."

"Determination and conviction, surely. But passion? That might not be something every lady can afford."

That, Meredith could understand.

Who was she to advise someone as wise as Lady Belfort? Yet Abigail could not help her feelings. One could have a passion for a project—her father certainly had—but that didn't make the project right for everyone else. Sometimes such a passion excluded all others. And that was seldom good.

Finn and Fortune returned just then. "Mrs. Landry says dinner will be served at six, if that pleases your ladyship," he said.

"Thank you," Meredith told him. She shoved back the letters as if she could not bear to look at them again.

Suddenly, Fortune darted through the open door.

Finn cocked his head. "Sounds like a carriage." He straightened and turned to Meredith. "Were you expecting visitors, my lady?"

"No," Meredith said. "But, as you noticed, we are not as thin of Society as some might expect. Jane, perhaps?"

"Perhaps. Excuse me." He left them for the entry hall.

Abigail could not be concerned. Neither the Bow

Street Runner nor the little spy would arrive in a carriage asking to be received. And she no longer associated with anyone with a carriage, except Meredith.

A few moments later, male voices echoed down the corridor. Fortune scampered into the library and squeezed behind the desk.

Meredith frowned.

Finn came in first and took up his position along the wall, back straight. His gaze might appear distant, but Abigail knew he was cataloging every movement, every word, alert for trouble.

Alert to protect her.

"Lord Granbury, your ladyship," Mr. Cowls said before stepping aside.

Abigail sucked in a breath as her former employer strolled into the room. Tall, powerfully built, with raven hair combed back from a long face, he was a master at showing the ennui of his class. She wasn't surprised when he inclined his head as if already bored by his visit.

"Lady Belfort. Thank you for receiving me."

"Lord Granbury," Meredith said. "I do not believe we have met, although I know you are acquainted with my companion, Miss Winchester."

His deep-set blue eyes swept over Abigail and brightened. "Indeed." He was obviously so sure of his welcome that he crossed the room and took the chair opposite her without Meredith's invitation. "And I am certain it is an oversight that you and I have not met, Lady Belfort. I have spoken with your good husband about matters for the crown."

If so, that was certainly news to Abigail. She had spent more time with the baroness than the baron, but Lord Granbury had struck her as the grasping sort under all that posturing. Coming late to his title, he clung to its trappings with one hand while reaching up for more, in wealth, in connection, in prestige. Why speak of dealings with a solicitor? Then again, Lord Belfort was no mere solicitor, or he would never have earned his own title.

"A shame Julian is traveling, then," Meredith said. "Perhaps we can renew the acquaintance when we return to London."

Another fellow might have taken the hint and bowed himself out. Lord Granbury crossed one booted foot over the other and leaned back as if prepared for a long coz. "That would be delightful. Do you expect him back shortly?"

Meredith did not smile as she came to join them, the swish of her lavender skirts loud. "When the negotiations are completed with Württemberg. Dealing with kings and princes can be so tiring, wouldn't you agree, Mr. Huber?"

If he was surprised to be brought into the conversation, Finn did not show it. "Indeed, your ladyship."

Lord Granbury acknowledged his presence with no more than a flick of his hooded eyes. "I am certain Lord Belfort's work will be fruitful. Which brings me to the reason for my visit. You have something I would very much like returned to me."

Meredith frowned. "I think not."

He aimed a smile at Abigail. "My daughters have been disconsolate since your departure, Miss Winchester." The smile found Meredith again. "I would cite their need as greater than your own, madam. You and your husband were not blessed with children, if I recall. Surely we can come to some sort of agreement."

He would bargain for Abigail as if she were a bit of ribbon his daughters coveted? The nerve of the fellow!

"We have no children," Meredith said. "But Abigail has become like a daughter to me. Naturally, I must consider what is best for her." She turned to Abigail. "Did you wish to continue in a position with Lord Granbury, my dear?"

Once she had been thankful for the position. Lord Granbury's home was luxurious, his daughters surprisingly sweet natured and clever. She had rubbed along nicely with the staff and Lady Granbury. Meredith seemed to think Abigail had mistaken the conversation that had driven her from his home. Did she want to return to London, take up her former post? Would she be safe from those who had been asking after her? It would certainly make things easier for Meredith.

And Finn.

She glanced his way, but his gaze was on the middle distance again, and she wasn't sure he saw her either.

Fortune strolled around the base of the chair as if she had nothing better to do with her time. Hopping up onto Abigail's lap, she glanced at the baron, then Abigail, then settled herself onto Abigail's skirts, putting her back squarely to their visitor.

Meredith raised a brow.

"No, thank you," Abigail said, the lightness inside her confirming her choice. "I am quite content where I am." She ran a hand along Fortune's back and received a purr for her trouble.

Lord Granbury tugged on his lapels. "I am prepared to raise her wages and provide larger living quarters, with her own sitting room."

His generosity failed to move her, particularly as he appeared to be speaking to Meredith again.

"Very kind," her ladyship assured him. "I'm certain your next governess will be appreciative. Have a safe journey back to London, my lord."

This time, he took the hint. He rose and inclined his head to her. "Lady Belfort. I hope next time we meet it will be under happier circumstances. Miss Winchester."

Her name sounded as cold as winter. Mr. Cowls saw him out.

Abigail glanced to Finn again to find him grinning. He

quickly snuffed it out, then moved to the door. "I will ensure he leaves."

"Thank you, Finn," Meredith said. As soon as he had left the room, she looked to Abigail. "Did you refuse because of Fortune's reaction?"

"In part," Abigail admitted, petting the silky fur. "But I cannot forget how we parted. He was all demand then. Why change now? It is as if he assumes I will fall upon his neck, rejoicing in my good fortune."

Fortune glanced up expectantly.

"Little humility," Meredith agreed. "But of course humility would be too much to ask of Lord Granbury, I sense."

"Precisely," Abigail said. "In short, I am well satisfied with my current position and your skills at finding me the right direction for the future."

"I can certainly do better than that offer," Meredith said with a look out the door, as if she could still see Lord Granbury's stiff spine as he departed.

CHAPTER TEN

TRY AS SHE might, Abigail could not put the visit from Lord Granbury out of her mind. The Bow Street Runner had told Finn someone had hired him to look into her activities. She could not imagine Lord Granbury putting himself to such expense for someone as minor as her. The very fact that he had come all the way to Surrey to find her was odd enough!

Finn and the other guards remained on alert as well, especially when they drove with Meredith and Abigail to the village for services on Sunday. Once again, she felt every gaze on them as they walked up the center aisle to Meredith's pew. Still, the familiar songs and readings settled over her like a warm blanket. The minister's sermon, however, brought back winter's chill.

"I had intended to read a sermon appropriate to the season," he said, peering at them all from his place at the front. "And you know I abhor the practice of bringing up momentary matters when we should be focused on the eternal. However, news from London is so troubling that I felt I must dwell on it. It seems some are still bent on making their own heaven on earth, quite aside from our Holy Father's decrees. I speak of this nonsense with Poyais."

Breath caught in her chest. Finn's hand reached out and held hers, anchoring her. She managed to return the smile to her face.

"Advancement far beyond one's station in life, income widely disproportionate to the effort involved, riches for the taking!" the minister scolded. "Those facts alone should have warned off our brothers and sisters from this nefarious scheme. Yet they ran after gold and privilege, with no heed of the consequences to themselves or their families. And they paid the price for it with their lives. Now we have word that the ultimate scoundrel, this Colonel MacGregor, has been apprehended in France, seeking to take in our neighbors across the Channel with the same scheme. Who next?"

She clutched the rail of the pew before her with her other hand, even as the dark crept in on all sides. No! She would not faint. She had done nothing wrong!

Finn's hand squeezed, and she glanced his way. His gaze was firm, constant. He would not let her drown in sorrow and guilt. As the minister droned on and on about humility, contentment in life, and care for one's brother, he remained at her side, comforting her merely by his presence. He did not judge her. And neither would God.

Still, her legs were decidedly shaky as she stood at the end of the service. As if he knew, he threaded her arm through his and gave her a game smile. Meredith went first, head high, and the other guards formed a phalanx around Abigail as they followed. All she wanted was the carriage and a little peace. She barely managed a pleasant nod in the direction of the duchess, who was watching with concern on her round face, and Miss Hewett, who looked disappointed not to have a moment to chat.

Mrs. Bee, however, seemed determined that none of them should escape unscathed. She and her daughters were waiting just outside in the cool autumn sunlight.

"There you are, Lady Belfort!" she heralded. Her younger daughter fluttered her lashes in the direction of the Imperial Guards. The older dropped her gaze to the ground, cheeks pinking.

"Mrs. Bee," Meredith acknowledged, though she did not stop moving. "Forgive me. I have an urgent matter that requires my attention."

"Certainly, certainly," the lady said, keeping pace with her so well her sunny yellow skirts flapped. "I will only take a moment. I merely wanted to ensure you will be attending the assembly on Friday."

Finn switched sides, inserting himself between Abigail and the woman. Roth did the same for Meredith.

"Of course," Meredith said around him, crossing the churchyard with remarkable speed.

"I do hope we might see your guests as well," Mrs. Bee said, and the youngest daughter, who was scampering along beside them, giggled while the elder hung back more shyly. "The assembly can be so thin when it comes to the company of charming gentlemen."

"We will be certain to save a dance for you," the youngest daughter put in with a look to Tanner.

"We do not dance," Roth said, shoving a shoulder between them so they might reach the coach.

Both daughters gasped.

"Oh, he is teasing," their mother said with a wave of her hand. "All gentlemen dance. I'm sure one of you will be escorting Lady Belfort, but I see no reason why the other three might not escort some of our local ladies. It is always pleasant to be seen on the arm of a gentleman in uniform. Mr. Keller for Elspeth, my oldest, perhaps, and Mr. Tanner for Angelica, the younger. As my husband does not care to attend, I shall take Mr. Huber."

The older daughter shrunk in on herself, but her sister's smile was knowing.

Abigail's hard-won composure took flight, and she didn't attempt to call it back. She stopped to glare at the woman.

"You are mistaken, Mrs. Bee," she said as Keller handed Meredith into the coach. "Mr. Huber has already agreed to escort me. And he and his colleagues are so necessary to their professions that they have no time for frivolous pursuits. You do them an injustice if you think otherwise. Good day, madam."

Finn found himself grinning as he settled beside Roth in the carriage. He would never forget the look on Mrs. Bee's face when Abigail had stood up for them. He wasn't sure what had shocked the lady most—that a companion would dare speak so fervently in company or that a lady would take the part of a guard.

"You will likely have to pay for that," Lady Belfort told Abigail as the coach set off. "But I would have given a guinea to watch you do it."

Abigail's smile was soft even as her cheeks pinked. "I fear I would do it again all too easily." Her smile faded. "It was the sermon."

Lady Belfort covered her hand with her own. "The minister's points were well taken. Too many were fooled by Colonel MacGregor. He wasn't singling you out."

"I know," she murmured, dropping her gaze. "But the subject is still of some concern to me."

To others too. He wished he knew how to ease her pain.

Unbidden, Lady Giselle's face appeared in his mind. He still remembered the day they had parted. Framed against amethyst bougainvillea climbing up the creamy stone wall of the palace King Frederick had let in Italy, her hair had stood out thick and gold, curling around her oval face. Her dark blue eyes had been brimming with tears, like a pool at the base of a mountain waterfall.

"It is impossible, Finn," she had lamented. "My father will never bless our union, not after that business with Karl."

He'd forced himself not to cringe at the reminder of his disastrous display. "I will do better. I will not fail you or your family again."

"No," she said with a heavy sigh. "Father is determined to remove you from your position. We have no choice but to part." She held out her hand, fingers dangling.

He was clearly expected to bow over it, perhaps press a kiss against her knuckles. Did she think his love so feeble he could snuff it out like a candle flame?

"If we stand united," he started.

Her hand had turned, rising in a clear sign to stop—his discussion, his hopes, his dreams, his love. "No, Finn. It is over. I must think of my future."

A future without him. The cut had been sharper than a saber slash. King Frederick had not yielded to the demands of Giselle's father to see Finn dismissed, but the unpleasantness made it clear he would never be welcome to return to Batavaria when the others did.

But now? He could only wonder whether it had been for the best. He would never have measured up in the eyes of her and her father. He could imagine himself striving for more, taking greater risks, perhaps compromising his character, all in the hopes of winning their respect.

Here, he was already respected. Lady Giselle would never have stood up for him the way Abigail had.

But that didn't mean he should consider her smitten. She had said it herself, and he had felt it. The sermon had dug its claws into her, probing parts still tender. Mrs. Bee had chosen to be demanding at the wrong time.

He had to remember he was only Abigail's bodyguard, even if a part of him persisted in wishing for more.

If Finn thought Abigail had spoken too forcefully to Mrs. Bee, he did not speak of it. Indeed, the smile playing about his mouth as they rode back to Rose Hill said he was rather pleased about the entire affair. She certainly could not regret it. He and the other guards deserved to be seen as individuals, not a new gown that would show off its wearer to advantage.

"I expect you all for dinner tonight," Meredith told the guards as they disembarked at the house. "Five. No need to dress."

Roth, who had the day off, saluted her. "As you wish, my lady." Turning, he frowned at Tanner and Keller. "Huber will be on duty. Drills at one for the rest of us."

"If you are going to spend the day studying," Meredith said, "you would be better advised to spend it with Abigail, learning how to comport yourself in an English drawing room."

"We will not be employed in English drawing rooms," Roth protested.

"That, you do not know," she reasoned. "And you would benefit from some polish, if the reports from your interviews are to be believed. One of the clock, as you noted, in the library, sir." She headed for the house.

"Were you expecting this?" Finn asked as he and Abigail followed.

"No," she admitted. "I was under the impression I wasn't needed after all. But I have until one to prepare."

He patted her shoulder as if in commiseration, then strode into the house to confirm all was safe.

When she had been a governess, she had often spent an hour or so each evening after her charges were in bed to go over the lessons and schedule for the next day. Now, as Finn stood along the wall, she sat with Meredith in the library and tried to think through what would be most useful for the guards to learn. They had been working with royalty—they must know the basic requirements of rank and etiquette. What more could she teach them to help them advance in their new home?

Roth, Tanner, and Keller returned to the house promptly at one, as ordered, and joined them in the library. Meredith captured Fortune and kept her on her lap, as if protecting the guards from her attempts to gain their notice. They stood at attention with Finn along one wall, bookcases behind them. She might almost believe they were holding the things in place, so still were they.

"Gentlemen," she said. "I am not your commanding officer. You are welcome to sit in my presence."

Keller looked to Roth.

"We will stand," he said.

"You see the problem," Meredith said to Abigail.

She nodded before looking back at the guards, trying to focus on Finn, who was watching her. "You are very skilled at being unseen. Your role has been to support from the shadows, like a lower servant. But you are not necessarily going to be employed as lower servants. A tutor, like a governess, is of a different class, and a bodyguard can be as close as a lady's maid."

Tanner cocked a grin, but a look from Roth knocked it off his face.

"I see two scenarios at which you must excel," Abigail continued. "The first is the interview. The second is general company. Let us start today with the interview. Sit down."

They must have been more comfortable with the direct command, for they all seated themselves in the chairs by the hearth and looked up at her expectantly. Finn's smile buoyed her.

"Now then," Abigail said, clasping her hands before her, "your interviewer may well be a gentleman or a man of means—either the master of the house or the owner of the establishment. He may find your size and experience admirable, but he will expect two things from you. Mr. Keller, can you guess one of them?"

"Humility," he said. "He will not want someone who will look down on him."

Roth raised a brow. "At more than six feet each, we look down on most men."

"But you must not act as if you consider them beneath you," Abigail countered. "Mr. Keller is correct. You must approach them with humility, but you must not grovel. Mr. Tanner, can you guess the other characteristic that will be expected?"

"Good humor?" he asked, crossing one booted foot over the other. Finn shook his head.

"No," she said with a smile, "though I will own good humor will see you through much in life. Mr. Roth?"

"Obedience," he said. "Just as any officer should expect from those under him."

"Correct. Although you should question him if he issues a request you do not understand or cannot meet. Shall we practice?"

Tanner dropped his foot to nudge Finn with it. "You go first."

Finn eyed him a moment, then turned his attention to Abigail. Lamplight highlighted the curve of his cheek. Dark lashes flickered over golden eyes as he blinked, waiting.

Oh, right. She was teaching!

"Pretend I am a gentleman interviewing you for a position as bodyguard." She raised her chin. "Mr. Huber, tell me what experience you have for the role."

"I have guarded His Royal Highness and His Majesty, the crown prince and king of Batavaria, for some years. Recently, I have been guarding a young lady from danger."

Abigail wrinkled her nose. "Probably best not to mention me, unless they're hiring you to guard a family or a wife."

He frowned. "He will say such things to me?"

She shook her head. "Sorry. I'll remain in character." She drew herself up again. "Excellent qualifications. Do you have letters of recommendation from your employers?"

"I do. I have left them with your secretary."

Nice touch. "And why should I trust you with my person?"

"Because I will do everything I can to protect you. I will not eat until you eat. I will not sleep until you sleep and even then not until I know another trusted person is watching over you. I will ensure every space is safe for you to enter, before you enter it, and you will have the comfort of knowing that someone watches over you at all times, looking out for your best interests. You will be my first priority, from the moment I wake until I am relieved of duty."

Goodness! She'd certainly hire him. But then again, she had.

"Excellent," she said. "The position is yours."

He smiled, and the sun came out, and birds sang, and all was right with the world.

"It is not so easy," Roth said. Was he determined to always see the dark? "What if they are suspicious of us as foreigners?"

Keller nodded. "Or doubt our credentials."

"The latter is more easily assuaged," Abigail allowed. "You will have letters of recommendation from the prince and Meredith, and the duchess offered them as well, so that should prove your claims. As to being foreign, it might be best not to take a position where your employer is already suspicious of you. You might end up being blamed for something."

Meredith spoke up at last. "And I will do all I can not to send you to such a place."

Encouraged, Abigail took a turn with each of them. Keller was eager, Roth wary, and Tanner the least likely to play along. But, overall, she was pleased by how quickly they caught on.

Meredith rose. "We will try more tomorrow. For now, I think a walk would do me and Fortune good. Abigail and Finn, join us."

Finn had seen Abigail serve as governess before, at the duke's house party, so he wasn't surprised how easily she explained things. Perhaps, with a little help from her, they all might find good positions with purpose.

As it was, strolling through the trees and shrubbery in the front garden felt wrong, as if he were neglecting his duty. Fortune seemed to agree. She kept rubbing her collar along the shrubbery, as if hoping to tear it off.

"Excuse me," he told Abigail, and he set off around the pond, gaze veering from the shrubs to the trees to the distance. Yet he spotted nothing unexpected. The clouds were gathering and the wind rising, promising rain.

As he came around closer again, Abigail put herself in his path. The blue pelisse hugged her curves, as if the sky had come down to embrace her, and the wind had put a bloom in her cheeks.

"Still concerned about unwelcome visitors?" she asked.

"Yes," he allowed. "We were surprised before, and in this spot." He glanced up into the oak, but no one looked back this time.

"You cannot help yourself, can you?" she said with a smile. "You simply have to protect. It's as if the urge is in your blood. Or is it the way you were trained?"

"We were all trained to protect the king, his sons, and the other members of his court," he admitted. "Yet duty is more than a shirt I put on in the morning. It isn't easy to take off. And it is what I do. Would you ask Wordsworth to lay down his pen?"

Abigail laughed, and the joy of the sound made his own lips rise. "I did think you a poet with the sword, sir. But even a poet must sleep and eat and enjoy the company of friends."

"I can do all that when we know you and Lady Belfort are safe," he told her. "I couldn't protect my family. I will protect those I love now."

She stared at him.

Why had those words come out? He knew better than to let his attention wander, even in conversation. Now, there was no denying the implication. His feelings were building, for all he had tried to prevent them. Best to retreat and regroup while he could.

"I must check the drive," he muttered and strode off faster than if the French cavalry had been nipping at his heels.

CHAPTER ELEVEN

DID FINN KNOW what he had just implied? He was yards away before Abigail could open her mouth to ask.

She nearly called him back. What would it be like to tell him she admired him too? To feel those strong arms come around her, those firm lips press against hers? To know herself cherished?

Joy bubbled up like steam from a teakettle.

She could not give it vent. He was trying to find a position, start a new life. Like Preston, he would find success difficult with a wife at his side riddled by scandal.

Isn't that Abigail Winchester, the daughter of the banker who financed the sailing of all those ships that took people to their deaths? How can she stand there, pretending she didn't know, pretending she wasn't involved? To the gallows!

She shuddered. So deep were Colonel MacGregor's sins that it would be years before his victims would be able to look at his associates with anything less than contempt. The minister's sermon today proved as much. All those people, all their hopes.

All their money. Gone.

So, she would not inflict herself on a good man like Finn Huber. She would not inflict herself on any man. She would find a way to make a life for herself, away from London Society. In time, they might forget.

Even if she never could.

She did not have an opportunity to speak privately with Finn before the others descended on them for a succulent dinner of roast beef with mushroom sauce, Yorkshire pudding, and salad. Conversation veered from events they had attended in London to autumn weather in Surrey. At last, Roth lay down his fork and directed his gaze at Meredith at the head of the table.

"Do you expect us to attend this assembly on Friday?"

"I would prefer it," Meredith admitted. "Though not in the company of Mrs. Bee and her daughters."

Abigail looked to Finn. He was watching her from across the table, candlelight flickering in his golden eyes. Was he wondering how well she might acquit herself on the dancefloor? She could certainly imagine herself spinning around the room in his arms. It would only be a dance. Surely she could protect her heart and his.

"Then we will go," Roth said with a look to the others that brooked no disobedience. "Those of us who are not employed by that date."

Meredith nodded her thanks, but she had paled as she reached for her goblet, and Abigail thought she knew why.

"You will find them positions," she told her benefactress that evening as they sat in the library after the others had left. Tanner would be spending the night and was making his final rounds.

"I certainly pray as much," Meredith said. "I would not have thought it so difficult to place four handsome, skilled, honest fellows! Ah, well. It is a new week. We will persevere. Now, let us talk about what you plan to wear to the assembly."

"I have no idea." She rubbed the thin fabric of the muslin gown she'd worn for dinner. "As you may have noticed, I only kept a few gowns I thought would be useful as a governess, and most of them are too light for an autumn evening. I have two wool gowns and a dinner dress as well, but none are suitable for a ball."

Meredith eyed her, head cocked. "I am not quite the size I once was, which was more aligned with yours, but I believe I have one or two gowns in the attics, waiting in hope I might have use of them again. We should have time to alter one for you."

Tears pushed against the back of her eyes. "Oh, Meredith, that would be wonderful. You are too kind."

"Nonsense," she said, though pink crept into her cheeks. "I am trying to find you a position, if you recall. It would not do to have you appear in public looking like a dowd. We will unearth the offerings in the morning and set to work on one immediately."

Abigail smiled her thanks.

Meredith's memories proved true, for they discovered a pink silk gown in a trunk the next morning, pink silk rosebuds at each corner of the square bodice and at the tip of the scalloped short sleeves. As Meredith now wore only lavender, the gown must have dated from when she had still lived with her mother in this house and been known as Mary Rose. The hem was marred in two spots, as if someone had trod upon it, but Meredith gave her yards of rose satin ribbon that Abigail could lay down in rows along the hem to cover the frays.

First, however, she must keep her promise to the guards.

They all met with her and Meredith in the upstairs withdrawing room this time. Abigail had thought it more conducive to practicing good behavior in polite company. But Roth stood in a corner. Keller hesitated, then slid in beside him along the paneled wall. Finn took up his place by the window.

Tanner sat on a chair near Meredith and leaned back as if prepared to enjoy the performance.

"Lesson one," Abigail said from her place before the hearth. "A gentleman never sits while a lady is standing, unless she has given him leave."

Roth smirked as Tanner climbed to his feet.

"Forgive me, Miss Winchester," he said with a bow so deep it ruffled his chestnut-colored hair. "I merely wanted to give you my full attention."

"Commendable," she said, fighting a smile at the excuse. She looked to the others. "I will remain standing for these lessons, but you may be seated, gentlemen."

Roth nodded to Keller, and the two found chairs. Finn elected to perch beside Meredith on the sofa, but his head was cocked, as if he was listening for something. The sound of a carriage, perhaps?

"When a lady stands," Abigail said, with a look to Meredith, "you stand."

Meredith rose gracefully. Roth and Keller shot to their feet. Tanner levered himself up more leisurely. Finn stood at attention.

"Very good," Abigail told them all as Meredith returned to her seat and the others sat as well. She caught Keller watching Meredith as if expecting her to pop up again at any moment.

"You already know to open doors for a lady and hand her in and out of carriages if no footman is available," Abigail said. "I have appreciated that courtesy."

"It is only your due," Tanner said, and Finn's eyes narrowed.

"However," she continued, "I have noticed that you can be rather brusque when conversing."

"Words are at an economy when danger threatens," Keller protested with a look to the others as if for support.

"Not every situation is dangerous, Mr. Keller," Abigail said, "regardless of what Mr. Roth might tell you."

Roth's sculptured cheeks reddened.

"Let us say you are not on duty and strolling along the

street in Weyton," Abigail tried. "You happen upon Lord Belfort, recently returned from his travels. What do you do?"

Once more, Keller shot to his feet. This time, he stood as straight as a broom handle and clapped his fist to his chest. "My lord. How might I be of service?"

"I'm sure Julian would be highly appreciative," Meredith put in. She looked to Abigail. "Perhaps we should use someone they would consider an equal as an example."

She should have thought of that. She had fallen into the same trap as the Bees, assuming them the equal of the royalty and aristocracy they served. But she could not see them on the same footing as a servant. Who did an elite Imperial Guard consider an equal besides one of their own?

"Nicely done, Mr. Keller," she encouraged him as he sank onto his chair, paling. "Mr. Roth, let us say you four have been working apart for some time, and you come across Mr. Huber while in London. What do you do?"

Roth stood, sleek as a panther she'd seen once in the Tower Zoo. His look to Finn was hard. "Huber. Report."

Tanner snickered.

Roth rounded on him. "What? Think you could do better?"

Tanner rose fluidly and stuck out his hand toward Finn. "Huber! Well met, old friend."

Finn stood and shook his hand. "Good to see you again."

Tanner grinned. "How are your daughters? I hear they look just like your dear wife, Abigail."

For a moment, Abigail lost her admirable composure, and Finn heard her suck in a gasp. Tanner had no right to tease her. He curled his fingers tighter around the guard's fingers and squeezed, hard.

"They are quite well," he answered, keeping his voice level. "A shame you could never find a lady willing to give you the time of day."

Tanner squeezed back, strong as a vise. "Not all of us are so fortunate. And the gout? I understand you can hardly walk at times."

Finn tightened his muscles, and Tanner grimaced. "Tolerable. Do they feed you at the Poor House?"

Finn's bones cracked audibly under Tanner's grip. "Very well, but that is only to be expected with me being the director. Did you ever straighten out that business with the vicar's daughter?"

"Very good, *gentlemen*," Abigail said in a voice every child must pay attention to. "You may both be seated."

Tanner disengaged, but he surreptitiously rubbed at his fingers as he resumed his seat.

Finn looked to Abigail. Her eyes flashed a warning before she pulled her usual composure back into place.

"Just remember to be polite and considerate," she said with a pointed look to Tanner. "Asking after mutual acquaintances and the other person's health and occupation are generally safe gambits."

"And there's always the weather," Lady Belfort added with a wry smile.

Finn sat beside her ladyship, who raised a brow at him. Fortune, who once more had been sequestered in Lady Belfort's lap, wiggled free and took possession of his lap instead. She brushed her head against his waistcoat, purr audible. His last bit of tension melted away.

"The next few lessons," Abigail said, "have to do with this assembly on Friday. It will likely be a little different from what you've seen with your king and prince. Am I correct in assuming all in the area are invited, Lady Belfort?"

"Any who can pay the six-shilling subscription," she said. "I will see that the amount is forwarded for you all."

Roth nodded his thanks.

"Then you will be expected to partner the ladies," Abigail told the guards. "However, you must remember that the choice of who to ask resides with you. You will find that some of the young ladies are quite adept at forcing the matter. Mr. Tanner?"

Tanner, who had been flexing his fingers as if trying to regain circulation, sat taller. "Ma'am?"

"Stand beside me, if you please."

Finn's spine straightened as Tanner strutted forward to stand next to Abigail. He cast Finn a glance of triumph. Fortune glared at him.

"Whatever I say," Abigail told him. "I want you to find a way to refuse to dance with me. Politely."

Tanner put a hand over his heart. "Why, Abigail, I would never refuse a chance to dance with you."

Finn heard a growl and glanced down at Fortune, but the cat was staring at him now as if rather concerned about the source of the noise herself.

"Very kind of you to say," Abigail replied. "Pretend I'm Miss Bee the younger, and beware of my sting." She started fluttering her lashes, leaned closer to Tanner, set her hand on his arm, and spoke in a childish voice. "Oh, Mr. Tanner, I do believe this is the dance you promised me."

"Alas, I must sit out," Tanner lamented, removing her hand. "Bum knee. An injury sustained protecting my country from French incursions."

Abigail ceased her posturing. "A plausible excuse, and nicely stated, but there are two possible problems with the approach. Mr. Roth, can you name one?"

Roth had had his head bowed, as if examining a button on his waistcoat. Now his gaze speared Tanner. "He lied. His knee was never injured in the war."

Tanner colored. "I was attempting to spare the lady's feelings."

"Always a wise choice," Abigail assured him quickly. "Though better if you can speak the truth as well. I was thinking, however, that the statement leaves open the possibility that Miss Bee will insist on keeping you company."

Tanner shuddered.

"I believe I know the other," Lady Belfort put in. "By claiming the need to sit out, you generally forfeit the right to dance with anyone else. Refuse one, refuse all."

Keller's eyes widened. "Then how can we escape Miss Bee and her sister?"

"By making an excuse, not a refusal," Abigail explained. "Mr. Roth could say he had promised to keep Lady Belfort company."

"Only if I had so promised," Roth muttered.

"Finn could say he must keep me in his sights," Abigail continued.

"Which I will most certainly do," Finn assured her. Color popped in her cheeks.

"I could say I had asked another lady for that dance," Tanner mused, "and then go find her."

"I could claim the need to visit the gentleman's retiring room!" Keller crowed.

Abigail's smile wiggled at the edges, as if she was trying not to laugh. "Very good, gentlemen. Now, how do we ask a lady to dance?"

Finn watched as she practiced with Roth and Keller. Tanner had no need for the skill; he could likely charm any lady who caught his eye. Finn had no need to practice either. He couldn't keep Abigail safe while dancing with someone else, and he had no desire to dance with anyone but her.

Abigail finished her lessons by early afternoon, well pleased with her pupils' progress. Roth was less stiff, Keller more confident, and Tanner a bit more serious. Finn had excelled, of course.

But her success meant that she must attend to her other duty—serving as Meredith's companion, even to the point of accompanying her on visits. The lady had settled on returning Miss Hewett's visit that day. A brisk breeze blew a flurry of leaves across the drive as Finn helped them up into the carriage.

"It is a little distance south of Weyton," Meredith explained as the carriage bowled down a country lane. Cows in the fields raised their heads to eye them as they passed. Finn's gaze out the window was more watchful. Abigail struggled to see danger in the green fields rolling away from the river, the graceful stone bridges arching over its tributaries. Trees displayed their autumn finery in bursts of rust and orange and yellow. Having lived in London most of her life, she found the vista enchanting.

Miss Hewett's father had had his home built on the edge of Crown lands. A solid, square stone house, with massive urns in front of the stairs and smaller ones at each corner of the flat roof, it was set on lawns that ran down to a curving lake.

Footmen in black tailcoats and white powdered wigs held the carriage door and then the front door open for them, and a butler even more starched and proper than Mr. Cowls welcomed them into the marble-tiled entry hall. Finn glanced in the room off the hall and up the rosewood stairs.

"I doubt Mr. Hewett would approve of you securing his house," Abigail whispered to him.

"Very likely," he murmured back, and he did not sound pleased about the matter.

He followed behind them as the butler led them with measured tread to a withdrawing room on the first floor, where the heiress and Mrs. Daring were waiting.

Abigail had seen some very fine rooms in the duke's castle and at Lord Granbury's, but this was something else entirely. No pain had been spared in decoration or furnishing. Every wall was covered in flocked emerald wallpaper from the floor to the soaring ceiling, which was inlaid with gilded roses linked by plaster branches. The round carpet was woven to resemble a lakeshore much like the one that could be seen out the window, and the massive landscape painting over the white marble hearth was framed in gold. The entire room shouted the wealth of its owner.

Dressed in a spring green gown with a white collar, her fiery hair tamed back, Miss Hewett almost looked as if she were part of the decor.

"Lady Belfort, Miss Winchester," she declared, holding out hands to welcome them from where she sat on an emerald velvet sofa. "What a lovely surprise. I'm so glad to see you on such a blustery day."

"Dreadful weather," Mrs. Daring said from the chair beside her, with a sniff and a shiver that set the tassels on her shawl to quivering over her own dove grey gown. "You may well develop the ague."

"The sun was just coming out," Abigail assured her, taking a chair opposite their hostess. "It promises to be a lovely afternoon."

Mrs. Daring sniffed again. Did she doubt Abigail's word? She had only to look out the window at the clouds flying across a blue sky. Or maybe she thought Abigail shouldn't be so free in her conversation. She, like Mrs. Daring, was only a companion, after all.

She glanced at Meredith to see if her benefactress also thought Abigail had overstepped, but Meredith joined Miss Hewett on the camelback sofa with a pleased smile.

The heiress leaned closer and glanced around at them all. "Did you hear about the highwaymen? Is that why you brought Mr. Huber as guard?"

Finn had been pacing the perimeter of the room, as if trying to determine any place a villain might hide. Now he stopped and regarded their hostess. "Highwaymen?"

"Indeed," Mrs. Daring supplied, hitching her shawl closer. "Frightful business. We shall all be murdered in our beds."

"Hardly murder," Miss Hewett chided her. "Though I suppose you are wise, Meredith, to take precautions."

Finn looked as if he were about to burst, and Abigail thought she knew why. He was struggling to find a polite way to ask questions.

"What exactly happened?" Abigail asked for him.

CHAPTER TWELVE

MISS HEWETT LEANED back. "So, you hadn't heard. It was along the river road, not far from Rose Hill, Father said, just the other day. A carriage heading out from London toward Chertsey was stopped by three men wearing masks. They demanded the family strip off jewelry, then disappeared with it into the woods. Of course, the family notified the constable as soon as they came upon him, but it was too late. There was no sign of the villains."

Mrs. Daring shivered.

"Has the duke been notified?" Meredith asked. "He is the local magistrate."

"I'm sure he has," Miss Hewett said. "But as there have been no more sightings, the highwaymen remain at large."

"Another reason for you to stay close, Mr. Huber," Meredith called.

Abigail could only agree. A highway robber would get nothing from her, but he might assume anyone traveling in so fine a carriage as Lord and Lady Belfort's would have money and jewels to spare.

As if he agreed too, Finn went to put his back to the wall where he could likely see out the door to the landing, as if he expected the highwaymen to come marauding through the house at any moment.

"*Another* reason?" Miss Hewett asked, once again glancing among them.

Abigail's body tightened. Surely Meredith wouldn't spill her secrets!

"There are always reasons," Mrs. Daring said with a sigh.

"Indeed," Meredith allowed. She smiled brightly. "And how is your father?"

Oh, the dear! Abigail relaxed, but Miss Hewett blinked as if surprised by the change in subject. Still, she was too polite to question it.

"He is well," she said. "Rather full of himself, truth be told."

Mrs. Daring tsked. "Mr. Hewett is determined that Julia make a showing at the assembly on Friday."

"Silly of him," she said, before either Meredith or Abigail could respond. "It's a local affair. It isn't as if anyone important will be there, with the exception of you two, of course."

"Well, we shall be glad to see you there," Meredith assured her. "I always enjoy the assemblies. Do you like to dance, Abigail?"

"Very much," Abigail said, preventing herself from glancing at Finn from sheer force of will. "There's such a rhythm to it. It makes one feel positively graceful."

"Like living a piece of poetry instead of reading it," Miss Hewett said.

"Exactly!" They shared a smile.

"Then I expect you both to be the belle of the ball," Meredith said with a fond smile.

Miss Hewett dropped her gaze to the lacy white cuffs on her gown. "And will all the guards be attending?"

"Any that do not have positions," Meredith said. She glanced at Abigail, who shook her head at this further demonstration of the lady's antipathy toward the Imperial Guards.

"Have they done something to offend you, Julia?" Meredith asked bluntly.

Her head jerked up, and her green eyes widened. "Certainly not. Why do you ask?"

"You seem to have an aversion to being in their company," Meredith observed.

"Perhaps it is merely the idea that one's life is so dangerous it requires constant guard," she said.

"I find the idea of a constant guard comforting," Mrs. Daring protested.

"So do I, Miss Hewett," Abigail admitted. Finn's presence tugged on her gaze like a magnet to filings, but she kept her face forward.

Miss Hewett held out a hand to Abigail. "Please, you must call me Julia, and I will call you Abigail. I feel we are destined to be good friends."

And how wonderful would that be! Meredith had been so kind, but Abigail could not forget that the lady was her employer. To have someone to whom she owed nothing but friendship would be very fine indeed, even if it only lasted while she was at Rose Hill.

"You honor me, Julia," she said, taking her hand and giving it a squeeze.

Julia beamed. "Not at all! We will both need allies at this assembly. Much as I adore dancing, I never enjoy the competition."

Abigail withdrew her hand. "Competition?"

"From Mrs. Bee and her daughters," Julia clarified. "They are certain they warrant the attention of every gentleman in the area. It has been that way ever since the younger Miss Bee came out earlier this year. You were fortunate to have missed it, Meredith. Even her mother defers to her now on occasion. I can only feel sorry for her older sister."

"Mrs. Bee's husband came late to his money," Meredith explained to Abigail. "A self-made man, fighting through adversity, which is always admirable. He seems more than happy to retire to his recently purchased manor and live out his good fortune with hunting and billiards."

"While she must make sure none of us forget they are one of the wealthiest families in the area now," Julia agreed. "She seems to think that wealth entitles her to whatever she likes."

"I imagine it does," Abigail said, "in many circumstances."

Mrs. Daring hitched up her shawl again. "She reminds me of a hornet, constantly buzzing about in a threatening manner."

"The Bees may buzz all they like," Meredith said with an airy wave. "I am convinced Abigail and the Imperial Guard are proof against them."

The next few days would put that theory to the test.

Tuesday, Mrs. Daring's dreadful weather appeared at last. Wind rattled the windows and sent rain sheeting across the garden. Abigail and Meredith holed themselves up in the library, while Finn prowled the corners as if he thought the storm might break through.

Abigail worked on her gown for the assembly while Meredith reviewed an inventory of stores from her cook.

"Applesauce, tomato ketchup, and no less than thirty-seven jars of pickled beetroot," she mused with a frown.

"Mother claimed it was good with turkey," Abigail consoled her, taking a stitch.

"Perhaps," Meredith allowed. She glanced up as Finn passed her desk for the door, Fortune at his heels. "Do you like pickled beetroot, sir?"

"No," Finn said, pausing to glance down the corridor. "But that was a carriage."

"In this weather?" Abigail looked to Meredith, whose face was paling.

"Go," Meredith told Finn.

And he was gone, shutting Fortune in with them. The cat dismissed him with a flick of her tail and stalked back toward Meredith. But, for once, Meredith's gaze did not seek out her pet.

Abigail set aside her sewing. "Meredith? What is it? What's wrong?"

Her normally unflappable employer shook her head, lips pressed thin.

The door burst open. Finn stormed in and shut it soundly before turning to eye them. Like Meredith, his face was pale.

"The Bees," he said. "Mr. Cowls would like permission to turn them away."

Meredith's chest rose and fell in a deep breath, fluttering the ribbons along her neckline. "No. They must have a reason for coming to us this way. Escort them to the withdrawing room. Abigail and I will join you shortly."

To his credit, he did not hesitate, though Abigail thought any true danger from Mrs. Bee and her daughters was to Finn and the other guards. At least, neither daughter could cry compromise with her mother in attendance.

As soon as he was out the door, Meredith scooped up Fortune in her arms.

"You expected something worse than the Bees," Abigail said.

She nodded, face close to her pet's. "If there were dire news from the Continent, the village postmaster would no doubt bring it. Every day I do not hear from Julian, I fear the worst."

It likely wasn't proper to hug an employer, but Abigail couldn't help herself. She went to slip her arms around Meredith, mindful of Fortune between them. "He'll write. He must know how important a letter would be to you after what you've been through."

She nodded again, back stiff, and Abigail disengaged.

"Thank you," Meredith said. She drew in a breath. "Now, let us see about our unwanted visitors."

Finn was up against the wall, literally and figuratively, as Abigail and Meredith entered the withdrawing room a few moments later. Miss Bee the younger was standing in front of him, chattering away, while his gaze focused on the distance, as if she were no more than a whining gnat. Even her older sister looked embarrassed by the display, her fingers knit together in the lap of her frilly lustring gown. Abigail thought his shoulders came down a little at the sight of her.

"Lady Belfort, how delightful," Mrs. Bee warbled, as if surprised to find the lady in her own withdrawing room. "Come, girls, and make your curtsies."

The older daughter rose from her chair and dropped a credible curtsey, but her sister abandoned Finn with ill-disguised annoyance to spread her skirts to Meredith.

"Mrs. Bee," Meredith said. "Girls. Please, join Abigail and me."

Abigail could only be thankful for her patroness. Meredith refused to allow any of them to forget her existence. As it was, the three hurriedly took their seats, as if they thought she might change her mind and order them out of the house if they didn't.

"Terrible weather," Mrs. Bee said, arranging her cranberry-colored wool skirts as if to ensure that the triple row of lace along the hem was all the more visible. "But I had promised my girls I would visit you today, and I am not one to forget a promise."

Her daughters smiled complacently.

"I'm surprised your coachman didn't counsel you against it," Meredith said. "Surely it endangered him and the horses as well."

Abigail could only hope Mr. Cowls was even now treating the fellow to hot cider while the horses enjoyed the shelter of the stable.

"He knows better than the question my judgement," Mrs. Bee assured Meredith. "You must be very firm with servants, Lady Belfort. If I've said it once, I've said it a dozen times. Isn't that right, girls?"

"Yes, Mama," Miss Bee the elder said with a nod that set her crimped curls to trembling. Neither daughter's hair had fared well with the rain, frizzing about their faces.

"And how are you doing with your dear husband gone?" Mrs. Bee asked, looking at Meredith as if she expected her to break down in tears any moment.

"Well enough," Meredith allowed. She patted Abigail's hand. "I have a good friend here to help me through."

Abigail smiled back.

"And such handsome escorts," Mrs. Bee agreed with a glance toward Finn. She focused back on Meredith with a smile that said she'd discovered a sale on good lace. "You really cannot keep them to yourself, you know."

"I have no intention of doing so," Meredith said. "They are in the process of finding new positions here in England."

"Positions with the king?" Miss Bee the elder put in, with an encouraging look to Finn.

"Very likely," her mother agreed before Meredith could speak. She patted her daughter's hand. "Until then, I'm sure they can be of use to all of us. Which have you chosen to partner my girls at the assembly?"

Would she persist?

"As Abigail so eloquently put it after services," Meredith said with a pleasant smile, "the guards may be too busy to attend. Indeed, Mr. Roth has already secured a position: as night watchman for the Thackery Steamworks."

The youngest daughter made a face. "The steamworks? But I thought he'd be squiring a marquess or a duke!"

So, that was their interest! Their father may have raised their stature into the gentry, but they hoped to marry a former Imperial Guard and find themselves swept up with the nobility. Had they never noticed their husbands would merely be standing along the wall, not eating at the table with the notables?

"Alas, such positions are few and far between," Meredith told them.

The youngest's face pinched as she glanced at Finn. "You mean they'll all be working at night, as no better than constables?"

Finn kept his gaze on the middle distance, but the planes of his face seemed to have hardened.

"I have hopes they will find good employment from employers who will value their unique skills," Meredith said.

"No doubt," Mrs. Bee said with a thoughtful look at Finn. "Some are certainly willing to pay for protection."

Her oldest daughter stirred. "Oh! They can protect us from the highwaymen."

"I take it you've heard the tale as well," Abigail put in, hoping to ease them onto another topic.

Mrs. Bee pressed a hand to the lace at her impressive chest. "To have such crime rampant in our very village is positively worrisome."

Abigail's relief was short-lived, for the lady turned her gaze once more on Meredith. "I'm sure you wouldn't mind lending us a couple of your gentlemen, Lady Belfort, just to ensure we reach home safely."

Abigail hoped Meredith would refuse, but she cocked her head, as if weighing the benefit of having the Bees leave sooner than later and exposing the Imperial Guards to their machinations.

"I believe Mr. Tanner and Mr. Keller might be available," she supplied.

At which point Mrs. Bee declared they had stayed too long and must away that moment. They waited only until a footman had fetched the two guards before climbing into their carriage, which their beleaguered coachman had brought around from the carriage house.

 Abigail tried not to laugh at the looks on their faces when both guards insisted on riding on horseback to accompany them instead of sitting inside the coach.

 "How did they think Mr. Tanner and Mr. Keller would return, if not by horse?" Meredith asked as the group headed out at last.

 "I wonder whether they intended the guards to return," Abigail said, smile winning free. "I rather think they'd hoped to keep them!"

 Finn could not envy Tanner and Keller. He could only think his friends wise to ride on horseback, even in the rain, rather than inside with the Bees. Still, it puzzled him. Why did two young women from a good family see him and his friends as candidates for marriage?

 The matter was so much on his mind that it tumbled out the next afternoon. Rain once more pattered against the windows, but the sound was softer, or perhaps he was merely becoming accustomed to it. Abigail and Lady Belfort were in the Great Hall, and Finn had positioned himself near Abigail, where he could see out the windows and the door to the entry hall.

 "Why do Mrs. Bee and her daughters pursue us?" he asked.

 "At least you did not have to flee the room," Abigail teased him as she thumbed through sheet music. Lady Belfort had charged her with making use of the spinet in one corner of the wide room. The lady herself was in another corner with her cook, discussing menus and winter stores.

 "I cannot understand," he told Abigail, who was seated

at the instrument's bench. "Surely her husband would protest their daughters marrying a guard."

"Marrying a former member of one of the most elite forces on the Continent," she reminded him. "I imagine they think you have been richly rewarded for your acts of valor and will continue consorting with royalty."

He snorted. "Your king has no use for us. And we have been so well rewarded we must now secure positions in a foreign country."

"But you have every hope for securing a position," she pointed out as she set aside a piece of music with a particularly complicated-looking line of notes. "One of the banks in London closed in April, and I understand others may be teetering. Some, like those who invested with Colonel MacGregor, have lost everything. A gentleman with experience and aspirations, not to mention connections in England and abroad, is much to be desired."

He could not fathom it. "Even by a lady?"

She cast him a glance from under her lashes. "Even by a lady, sir."

The mind boggled.

Mr. Cowls' phlegmy cough rattled against the paneling. Finn glanced up to find him at the door to the Great Hall, a slender younger man that Finn recognized as one of Lady Belfort's stable hands at his side.

"A word, your ladyship," the butler said, voice surprisingly strong for a change.

Fortune, who had been winding about the cook's skirts, as if hoping for a treat, left her to accompany Lady Belfort across the room. Finn swiveled to keep them in sight, unease curling through him.

"Is something the matter?" her ladyship asked.

"I will leave that for you to decide," Mr. Cowls said. "Young Pat, here, brought me a tale I can scarcely credit." He looked to the groom.

The fellow had already yanked the hat from his head and now twisted it in his hands. "I can scarcely credit it myself, your ladyship. I've never seen its like, and neither has my da, and he's been working for your family since he was a lad."

"I am well aware of your family's longevity in service," Lady Belfort said, as Fortune brushed against the fellow's legs. "What seems to be the trouble?"

He visibly swallowed before looking to Mr. Cowls again. The butler nodded encouragement.

Pat squared his shoulders. "I was on my half-day off, your ladyship, and I stopped by the public house for a pint. Fellow sidles up to me and offers to buy me a second. 'What for?' I asks him. 'I don't rightly know you.' 'But I know you,' he says. 'You work for Lady Belfort up at Rose Hill. And I'll pay you good coin to tell me the goings on there.'"

Finn stiffened. So did Abigail and Lady Belfort.

"What affrontery!" her ladyship declared. "To ask my own staff to spy on me."

"Not you, your ladyship," he said. He nodded to Finn. "Him."

Finn stared at him. He could think of only one reason for someone to seek information about him—to find a way to prevent him from protecting Abigail.

"Did he say nothing more?" Lady Belfort demanded. "Who had hired him? Why Mr. Huber in particular?"

The stable hand shook his head. "No, your ladyship. I probably should have thought to ask. I let him know I'm not the one to tell tales on my betters and to take himself off. I must have been louder than I intended, for some others weighed in then, saying how they thought quite highly of you and his lordship and didn't take kindly to anyone threatening you. He left right then."

"And you have no idea where he went?" Finn pressed.

"Sorry, sir. I was too glad to have so many at my back. We were all rather pleased with ourselves."

Abigail put a hand on Finn's arm as if to forestall the other questions that crowded him. "Can you describe him, Pat?" she asked. "That might help us know who is trying to trouble Lady Belfort."

"Small fellow, older," he said, gaze going up to the ceiling as if he could see the stranger even now. "Greying hair. Close-set eyes. Weasley set to his face. I should have known he was up to no good the moment he opened his mouth."

CHAPTER THIRTEEN

SO, THE MAN with the squinty eyes was back, and he had set his sights on Finn this time. He shook his head in frustration.

"You did very well to bring us the tale," Meredith told Pat. "And I will be sure to let Lord Belfort know how valiantly you and the others defended our honor."

The stable hand dropped his gaze and resumed fiddling with his hat, coloring. "Tweren't nothing, your ladyship."

Mr. Cowls nodded to him, and they left.

Lady Belfort picked up Fortune as if to keep her from following. "It seems you have garnered attention, Mr. Huber," she said, glancing his way. "We will have to remain vigilant."

Finn inclined his head. "I will do all I can, your ladyship. If you will pardon me a moment, I'd like to speak with the others."

He was all too aware of Abigail's gaze on him as he quit the room.

He found all three of his comrades at the cottage. Roth must have risen early and set the others to work, for they were in the room off the kitchen, polishing their boots, much to the chagrin of their footman, who clearly saw that as his task.

"So, someone is watching you," Roth said after Finn had told then the stable hand's story. "And through you, us."

"And Lady Belfort and Miss Winchester," Tanner reminded him, giving his boot an extra rub, then tilting it to the light as if to admire himself in the reflection.

"I am more concerned that he singled me out," Finn confessed. "Why watch a bodyguard, unless you hope to distract or prevent him from his work?"

"Could it have been the same fellow we caught in the tree?" Keller asked, setting his boots carefully on the floor.

"The description sounds similar," Finn allowed. "But there's been no other sign of him lately. Where has he been, if not in the village? And why is he determined to watch us?"

None of them had answers, but they all agreed to remain alert, especially as the assembly neared. It had been ever thus. Standing along the wall in the state palace, with other guards within hailing distance, was one thing. Accompanying the king and prince into crowds was something else entirely. Their movements were harder to predict; the people approaching them less likely to be known in advance. A soldier must be ever on his guard.

This assembly would be worse. From what Lady Belfort had said, anyone with the subscription price to attend could come. Many would be able to afford the six shillings. Lady Belfort and Abigail would be mingling with people above and below their station. Friend would be hard to tell from foe.

Especially when his gaze wanted to linger on Abigail.

Over the next two days, while Finn and Keller watched the manor, Roth and Tanner patrolled the estate. They discovered a poacher, who Lady Belfort warned off, but no sign of anyone who appeared to be spying on the house. The weather was sufficiently bad that no others came to call. Abigail even entertained them all with a concert, her fingers pulling the notes from the old spinet with ease. It was as if they had returned to the Batavaria of his youth—peace and prosperity as far as the eye could see.

Finn could not trust it. Or, rather, he feared to trust himself. Every moment in Abigail's company, every soft smile, each gentle word, and he felt his defenses crumbling like a castle wall under a barrage from French cannons. But he could not keep her safe if he could not focus on his duty.

"Dress uniforms tonight," Roth ordered when Finn returned to the cottage on the evening of the assembly.

Keller looked up from the book he had been reading in the sitting room. "Are we allowed to wear our uniforms?"

"It was never forbidden," Roth reasoned. "And what better way to make a show of force?"

Finn couldn't argue with that, though he wished the older guard could have gone with them instead of to his job. Still, perhaps wearing the familiar uniform might help him remember why he was there.

Unfortunately, the sight of Abigail on the stair when he returned to the house a short time later burned any thought of duty from his mind.

She had been working on her gown all week, and he had caught glimpses of soft pink silk and rose satin ribbon. But he had not imagined how the gown would drape her curves, from the swell of her breasts above the little rosebuds decorating the neckline to the hint of her swaying hips as she descended. Another silk bud was positioned at her left temple, next to the tendrils of gold that curled down from her upswept hair.

"Spring has deigned to grace autumn," he said, taking her hand and bowing over it, "and leaves us all in awe."

"I can only agree," Lady Belfort said, stepping down behind her in her own satin ballgown, lavender, of course, as was the turban on her dark hair.

Mr. Cowls came forward with the lady's evening cape,

and a footman held up one for Abigail. Finn took it from him and set it about her bare shoulders, his glove skimming the pearly skin.

Why had breath become so difficult? He had promised himself to remain on guard, against any enemy. Even against her.

Keller had lost the coin toss and rode on the roof with the coachman. At least the weather had cleared, with stars beginning to peek into sight in the twilight sky as they set out.

Tanner sat inside with Finn. He kept up a steady stream of gallantries as the coach headed for the west of Weyton, where the assembly rooms lay.

Though he felt Abigail's gaze on him from time to time, Finn kept his gaze on the passing view. The moon was still full enough that the road was clearly visible, though the trees were clothed in shadow. An entire army might have been hidden among them, waiting to attack. He caught himself tugging at the black jacket with its gold braid across the chest and forced his hand to still. Both the coachman and Keller were armed with sword and pistol, and Tanner had stashed a brace of pistols under the seat. If anyone thought to harm their ladies, the guards would be ready to defend.

He saw the creamy stone building well before they reached it, for lights blazed inside and out. Footmen who must have been borrowed from various local houses opened carriage doors, while grooms held horses, so that a glittering array of local gentry could alight. Tanner helped Lady Belfort down and led her toward the assembly rooms, while Finn assisted Abigail. Keller had already pushed past some of the other guests, to exclamations of indignation, and now returned with a nod to let them know it was safe to enter.

"Three rooms and the kitchens," he told Finn as he held open the door for him. "Ballroom is shaped like an octagon. Good vantage, but hard to defend. Supper room is long, narrow, and fairly open, but remains empty. Card room is square and tightly packed, and many are already seated. I cannot tell if they are armed."

"They are not armed," Lady Belfort said, glancing back at him over her shoulder as Tanner helped her off with her evening cloak. "The master of ceremonies would not allow it." She nodded toward an older gentleman who was warmly greeting each arrival.

Tanner leaned closer. "He would not notice if someone brought in a pistol."

Finn nodded.

Lady Belfort fluffed up iridescent sleeves that had been crushed by her cloak. "I do believe we are safe here, gentlemen. What would Mr. Roth say? Take your ease."

But he could not. The ladies made straight for the ballroom, which had walls the color of butter, with white molding in fanciful swirls. In an alcove over the door, musicians were positioning themselves and their instruments. He counted a dozen footmen weaving through with goblets brimming with golden liquid. Too many opportunities for danger.

"This is impossible," Finn muttered as they found a place along the wall to wait for the dancing to begin and Lady Belfort introduced Abigail to this friend and that.

Keller leaned closer. "Not entirely. Remember when we were guarding Lady Moselle?"

Finn nodded, gaze sweeping the crowd. "Every time she attended something like this I worried."

"There is a trick to it," Keller murmured. "Never leave her side."

Finn regarded him. "How am I to do that when she is dancing?"

Keller grinned. "By being her partner."

Heat and cold swept over him in turns. He made himself scowl. "The English have rules for that sort of thing. Prince Otto Leopold chafed against them. No more than two dances for any one gentleman."

Tanner must have heard, for he sidled closer. "That's why we will all take turns. Two dances each, six dances total."

"Will that fill the evening?" Keller asked.

"Lady Belfort!" The local minister approached and held out his hands. "You grace us with your presence. Might I be so bold as to offer myself as a partner to your charming companion for the first dance?"

"Delighted, sir," Abigail said, and she sailed off with only a glance at Finn.

"We will have to be faster," Keller said with a shake of his head.

It wasn't easy. Finn claimed Abigail as soon as she came in from dancing with the minister, but not before Keller had been put in a position by the youngest Bee daughter to dance with her. Apparently he had forgotten Abigail's lesson on the matter. Another young lady had fluttered her lashes sufficiently that Tanner had succumbed as well. Finn could see them down the line, attending to their partners. Which meant they were not attending to their duty.

"It is only a dance," Abigail reminded him as if she had noticed his gaze moving.

"It starts with a dance," he allowed.

Then the music began. She curtsied, and he bowed. He had seen this particular dance in Germany and England, so it wasn't hard to follow the steps and make sure he was in position to twirl her, take her hands, or cavort down the set. He must watch for any danger, yet how could he fail to admire her lithe step, the joy that lit her eyes. The little rosebuds bobbed as if bowing before her beauty. Every fellow they passed smiled in appreciation.

It would be a challenge to hand her over to Tanner or

Keller for the next dance. He wanted to keep her close, bathe in the golden smile.

How had he come to this pass again, to care for a lady who made attending to duty so difficult?

Oh, to drink in the admiration in his gaze! Every time Finn glanced her way, smile hovering, she knew herself beautiful. Her heart danced as joyously as her feet.

A shame propriety demanded that she only award him two dances. Keller took her hand the moment the dance ended. He was an athletic partner, being particularly good at the leaps, which elicited cries of delight from the ladies. Tanner, the next to partner her, liked to put in little flourishes with his toes and hands that made her beam. But Finn, Finn was strength and grace and an economy of movement that was elegant and refined. Controlled. She understood the need for control.

So she engineered it that he was her last partner before supper was called, giving her the excuse of going in on his arm. Keller escorted Meredith, and Tanner came behind, alone.

"There's Julia," Meredith said with a nod.

Somehow Abigail had managed to miss her friend. She turned a smile in Julia's direction now, but Julia put her back to them and went in to supper with Mrs. Daring and an older man who must be her father.

"Perhaps she didn't notice us either," Abigail said as they found a table near the back.

"Very likely," Meredith agreed. She smiled around at the guards. "Though I cannot see how. Every lady here tonight is envious of our escort."

Tanner tipped his chin in acknowledgment of the compliment. Keller blushed.

"You are too kind, your ladyship," Finn said. "But we

are the fortunate ones to be escorting the most beautiful ladies at the ball."

Now Abigail was blushing.

The two other guards dug into the thinly sliced ham, baked mushrooms, and oysters, but she wasn't sure Finn ate a bite. Always, his gaze kept moving, as if watching for any darkness among the light.

Abigail lay a hand on his arm. "Surely we are safe here."

He covered her hand with his own. "I will make certain of that."

Though the program called for several more dances after supper, Abigail had no heart to partner anyone but Finn. So, she stayed by his side, and they walked around the edges of the room. She would have called it a promenade. She had no doubt he considered it a patrol.

On the second pass around the octagon, she sighted Julia just ahead, watching as an older gentleman requested Mrs. Daring's hand for a dance. Dressed in a peach satin that called attention to her fiery hair, she looked pleased to see her companion be given her due.

Abigail hurried forward.

"Julia! We haven't had a moment to speak all night."

Her friend started. Her gaze darted to Finn at Abigail's side, then her shoulders came down, and she smiled stiffly.

"You've been much in demand," she said. "Mr. Huber, I'm sure Miss Winchester is parched. Be so kind as to fetch her a glass of lemonade."

She clearly wanted a moment alone with Abigail, but Finn's face shuttered. "I regret that my duty…"

"Would be satisfied by a tour of the room," Abigail finished for him. "And you can secure the drink on your way back to me."

He regarded her a moment, then clapped his fist to his chest and stalked off.

"What is it?" Abigail asked her friend. "What's wrong?"

Julia beckoned, and they slipped back against the

butter-colored wall. The dowagers seated just down the way regarded them a moment before raising their fans and leaning closer to each other to gossip.

"I find myself in a difficult position," Julia murmured as the music started again. "My father is quite strict as to my acquaintances. There is one here tonight I would gladly recognize, but it might be difficult for us both should I do so."

Abigail started. "One of the Imperial Guards!"

Julia nodded. "Mr. Tanner. I did not know his name, mind you, until Meredith mentioned him."

"But you have me all intrigued!" Abigail leaned closer. "How can you know Mr. Tanner and yet not know his name?"

She worried the white silk of her evening gloves. "Before I attended the ball the duchess gave at her house party, my father and I had quarreled. I thought I could put the matter behind me, but it followed me to the ball and would not leave. I went out into the garden and had a good cry. Mr. Tanner came upon me then."

"Oh," Abigail said, beginning to understand.

"He was the utmost gentleman," Julia assured her, "but I knew what would happen should we be discovered together. I returned to the ball, but I never forgot his kindness. And now he is here, and I cannot even acknowledge him without alerting my father to the indiscretion!"

Abigail took her hand. "Allow me to introduce you formally, then. You can claim acquaintance later, if you wish."

She shook her head. "Not with my father here. I love him dearly, Abigail, but he has it in his head that nothing less than a duke will do for his daughter. He chases off every other man who shows interest."

Abigail made a show of looking left and right. "Alas, no unmarried dukes in sight."

Julia sighed. "Don't I know it. And I'm not sure I'd want one if he did suddenly appear!"

Finn shouldered his way past the crowd coming off the dancefloor, a glass of lemonade in each fist. "Ladies."

"Thank you," Abigail said, taking one and offering it to Julia.

Her friend was staring straight ahead, color flaming until her cheeks were the same color as her artfully curled hair.

Tanner bowed before them. "Miss Winchester. Would you be so good as to introduce me to your charming friend?"

Bless him! He must understand the danger as well. Finn was frowning, as if he sensed something was wrong. Or perhaps he thought Tanner too forward.

"I'd be delighted," Abigail said. "Miss Julia Hewett, may I present Mr…" belatedly she realized she didn't know Tanner's first name.

"Kristof Tanner," he said, clapping his fist to his chest in salute. "Your servant, Miss Hewett."

"Mr. Tanner." Abigail had never heard Julia's voice so faint, as if she could not find breath. "A pleasure."

"Might I hope that you would favor me with a dance?" he asked.

Oh, that would never do. Abigail stepped between them. "I believe you promised this dance to me, Mr. Tanner."

Julia put a hand on her shoulder. "It's all right, Abigail. I'd like to dance with Mr. Tanner."

Abigail blinked but moved out of the way. Tanner led her friend out onto the floor.

"What was that?" Finn asked, watching them.

"I'm not entirely sure." She took a sip from the glass. "But feel free to drink that lemonade. I don't think she'll be back for it any time soon."

He tipped up the glass, but his gaze was on the line of

dancers. Tanner and Julia were in the middle, watching as the first couple led off. Or at least, Julia was watching. Tanner was watching Julia.

"Tell her to be careful," Finn murmured. "He likes to flirt."

"I am not surprised," Abigail said, cradling her glass. "You, however, do not like to flirt. At least, I have seen you make no attempt to attract the ladies."

He took another sip before answering. "I learned flirting can lead to trouble."

"Only if the lady thought you insincere," Abigail assured him. "I would never assume you insincere, sir."

He handed his now-empty glass to a passing footman, then turned to her. Before she knew what he was about, he had taken her free hand and brought it to his lips. And she'd thought Julia breathless!

"Nor would I ever be insincere with you, Abigail," he murmured. "Despite my every effort, you have all my devotion."

She was so enthralled that she almost missed the fellow bearing down on them.

"Abigail," her one-time suitor Preston Netherfield said, stopping next to Finn and bowing. "At last I've found you."

CHAPTER FOURTEEN

HE SHOULD NEVER have taken his mind off his duty. Had he learned no lesson from Lady Giselle? This fellow had come near enough to harm Abigail, was even now standing far too close. Finn widened his stance and used his body to block any further forward movement.

The man was oblivious. All his attention was on Abigail. An inch or two shorter than Finn and more slender, he had an elegant cut to his face, his bearing, and his clothing. But true muscle and well-placed padding were easy to mistake. Finn would have wagered on the latter.

"Mr. Netherfield," she said, and the breathless quality of her voice hit Finn in the chest like a pugilist's fist. "I did not expect to see you here."

"Very likely," he allowed. "I have not set foot out of London in some years. But that should tell you how important this meeting was to me."

He did not say *she* was that important to him. Finn put a hand to Abigail's elbow.

At last the fellow registered his presence. He looked Finn up and down, golden brow raised. "If you please. I require a moment with my betrothed."

His betrothed? Was this the coward who had abandoned her when the scandal had hit? He squared his shoulders.

She sucked in an audible breath. "I am not your

betrothed, Mr. Netherfield. We made that decision some time ago."

"Then you are lost to me?" He glanced to Finn. "Has another claimed your love?"

She hesitated, and Finn's heart thudded in his ears. Would she say she had fallen in love with him? "Mr. Huber is not my betrothed," she said at last. "He is my bodyguard."

Netherfield reared back. "Your bodyguard? Why? Who dared accost you?"

Finn had been just as concerned when Abigail had first approached Lady Belfort, but he refused to give the fellow any more details than necessary. "That is none of your affair. My patroness, Lady Belfort, engaged my services to protect her companion and her."

"I… see," Netherfield said. He looked to Abigail. "It's this business with Poyais, isn't it? It has brought doom on us all, just as I feared."

She paled. "It feels that way at times. Did you lose your position at the bank?"

"No," he allowed. "My superiors have been pleased to keep me on."

"Then why come all this way now?" she asked.

His smile looked as if it had been painted in place. "I have come to realize what I lost. Allow me to make amends, preferably somewhere less public."

Finn threaded Abigail's arm through his. "Miss Winchester goes nowhere without me."

Netherfield drew himself up.

Abigail removed her arm from Finn's grip. For a moment, he felt empty.

"It's all right, Mr. Huber," she said. "I quite agree with you that any discussion with Mr. Netherfield should be held in public. The ballroom, in full view of all of Weyton's finest, would seem quite appropriate. I'm certain he would do nothing to jeopardize the reputation he has worked so hard to protect."

Netherfield glanced around as if noticing for the first time the number of gazes being directed their way.

Abigail looked to Finn. The quiet command he had so admired in the schoolroom was evident in the tip of her chin, the cool reason of her voice.

"If you stand just there," she said, "you can see both me and Mr. Netherfield. If anything should displease you about the conversation, you have my permission to intercede." She glanced to her one-time beau. "With force, if necessary."

There. If the threat of public censure had not daunted Preston, perhaps the threat of retribution would. She struggled to believe he had come to seek her out, after being so long from her side. Yet what other reason could he have for appearing at the Weyton assembly, of all places?

Beside her, Finn graciously inclined his head, sent Preston one last narrow-eyed look, then marched off to hold up the wall nearby. Abigail offered him a smile before turning to her former suitor.

"What are you doing here, Preston? You did not come all this way for me."

"Of course I did," he protested. "You are impossibly important to me."

Even with that fervent look on his handsome face, doubt was all too easy. "Indeed. I rather thought myself of far less importance than your career. Simply knowing me supposedly endangered your reputation."

His shoulders sagged. "I spoke from fear at our last meeting, and I have regretted it ever since. My reputation is vital to my career, but I am convinced it is well enough established that I should not have doubted our association could trouble it."

He thought rather well of himself. "You must have taken some trouble to find me."

"It was due penance. I started with your family solicitor, who said you had gone into service. I then went round to every employment agency asking after you. Finally one pointed me to Lord Granbury, who confessed you had left his service to come here."

He peered closer, as if he could see the stigma of service clinging to her like a cobweb. "You are a companion, Abigail? To which of these dowagers?" He spared a glance for the silver-haired ladies lounging along the wall. One wiggled her beringed fingers at him.

"The one dancing the waltz with such grace," Abigail said with a nod toward the dancefloor. Lady Belfort sailed past on Mr. Keller's arm, lavender skirts belling.

He frowned as if he thought she must be mistaken. "Why would such a lady require a companion?"

"Because her husband is presently traveling," Abigail supplied. "And I suppose she is lonely."

His frown cleared. "So it is a temporary position only."

"For now," she hedged. "I greatly enjoy Lady Belfort's company, so I hope she will consider keeping me on."

His look came back to her. "But why? You are not needed here. Surely she can spare you."

Abigail's spine stiffened. "Perhaps I don't want to be spared."

He took no notice of the steel in her voice. "Be sensible, Abigail. Marriage offers far greater advantages to a woman than servitude or spinsterhood."

Once she would have shuddered at the words, praying neither lay in her future. Now she had another future in mind.

"I suspect," Abigail said, "that depends on the marriage.

Besides, I do not recall you offering marriage, Preston. Our association had not reached that point."

He raised his manly chin. "And that fault may be laid at my door. I am too cautious by nature. I should have been bolder." He reached for her hands and held them tight. "Allow me to prove my devotion to you."

She should be looking as deeply into his eyes as he was into hers, but her gaze fled to Finn, standing along the wall. Waiting. Through wind and rain and tedious visits with the Bees. Ready to leap to her defense at the least sign. That was devotion.

And she doubted Preston could come anywhere near to matching it.

She pulled free. "Truly, sir, I cannot think of anything we have to say to each other. You have apologized. Your conscience should be clear. Let us agree to part as friends."

"Friends?" The word came out a yelp of protest. "Abigail, surely you know you mean more to me than that. I can understand that my appearance caught you by surprise. Promise me you will allow me to present my case more clearly."

She didn't want to promise him anything. He'd chosen duty to his family over love for her. Part of her wanted to see him suffer, at least a little. But that was not the person she wanted to be. With Finn at her side, Preston presented no danger. She would do him the kindness of hearing him out.

"Very well," she allowed. "Where are you staying?"

Again, he drew himself up. "You cannot visit me there. It wouldn't be fitting."

"I wasn't considering visiting you," she said, patience thinning despite her best intentions. "I merely thought to suggest that you ask your hosts about Rose Hill, Lady Belfort's estate. They should be able to point you in the right direction. She generally receives callers in the early afternoon."

"I would not presume to call upon Lady Belfort," he said, that tone she had never liked creeping into his voice. Preston had a strong sense of propriety and felt the need to instruct others in it on occasion. She had never fallen afoul of the trait, until now.

"Then I fear this is goodbye," she said equally primly. "I am her companion. I cannot accept callers on my own."

He shook his head. "You see how shabbily she treats you! I can offer you so much more." He reached for her hands again. Abigail twisted to one side, trying to avoid his touch. Another set of fingers latched onto his wrists like manacles.

"Take your hands off me, sirrah!" Preston demanded.

Finn maneuvered him skillfully to one side. "When you can convince me that you have no designs upon Miss Winchester."

Preston's chest was heaving. "My association with Miss Winchester is none of your affair."

Finn bent to meet his gaze. "Everything about Miss Winchester is my affair. I have sworn to protect her from anything and anyone who might do her harm."

"Do you dare accuse me of wishing her harm?" Preston asked, voice quavering.

The music had ended. More gazes were veering their way. So was Keller. Tanner deposited Julia with her companion, who stared at him, before following.

Meredith reached Abigail first. Her lavender gaze was especially sharp and only softened when she glanced her way. "Abigail, dear, you are not dancing. Finn, you must partner her."

"With pleasure," he said, and before she knew what he was about, he had swept her out onto the floor.

"That was badly done, sir," she said as they took their places across from each other for a country dance.

"I effect rescue where it is needed," he said, but there

was a light in his golden eyes that could only come from satisfaction.

She smiled. "And it was needed. I cannot imagine what possessed him to come after me."

He leaned forward. "I can."

Heat flushed up her even as the music swelled.

And as they danced, the world fell away again. Poyais, Preston, the Bees—what were they compared to this joy? Preston's hands had felt cloying. Finn's touch made her want to fly. She would not question beyond that at the moment.

As the dance ended, Abigail linked her arm in his. "Three dances, Mr. Huber? There will be gossip."

"I was under orders," he said, smile hinting.

"Ah, so it takes the order of your commanding officer to force you to dance with me," she teased.

He made no answer, as they were approaching Meredith and the others. She was surprised by how relieved she felt that Preston was nowhere in sight.

"Mr. Netherfield instigated an introduction," Meredith said, in the same tone as describing lancing a boil. "I expect he will attempt to call tomorrow. Would you like me to turn him away?"

It seemed as if every one of the guards held his breath for her answer. Finn's gaze held hers as well.

"No," Abigail said. "I will hear him out. And then I will send him packing."

Finn rode on the roof with the coachman on the way back to Rose Hill. The perch gave him a better view of the countryside, rimed in silver from the moon. The cool air penetrated even his uniform, but that was to the good. It kept him alert.

Still, he could not convince himself his duty forced

him here. Though he could not think well of Preston Netherfield's character after the way he had abandoned Abigail, the fellow likely lacked the courage to attempt a kidnapping. And there was better prey afoot for any highwayman.

No, he was riding here because if he rode next to Abigail, he might find himself saying things he had no business saying. He'd already said enough.

Devotion, he'd claimed, as if he were a pup she'd raised from birth. He had hoped at least to school his face, but she'd likely seen the admiration shining from it. It was only her due. A man would have to be mad to look on her with anything less.

Perhaps he had gone mad to think of a future together. With no title, no wealth, no permanent position, what had he to offer her? It was selfish of him to think otherwise.

So, tomorrow, he would remember his duty and strive to do it to the best of his ability.

Because honor demanded it.

Abigail had hoped for a moment alone with Finn before she retired, but he stayed on the roof when they reached the house and rode around to the stables. Keller was their guard for the night. He smiled apologetically, as if he knew she was hoping for someone else.

After the maid had helped her out of her finery, she lay in bed, the night tumbling past like views from a kaleidoscope.

Finn, dancing beside her down the line, power and grace combined.

Finn, taking her hands, promising her his devotion.

Finn, taking Preston's wrists, forcing him back from her.

Protecting, always protecting.

Could he tell she longed to do the same? To walk beside him, sharing stories, sorrows, and joys? To hold his heart as gently as he held hers? To encourage and support.

To love.

And yet, she could do none of those things. Reputation had driven Preston. Honor drove Finn. Marriage to a woman fleeing a scandal would never serve. She had lost him before she'd said a word.

Tears came, and for once, she let them fall.

As if in charity with her feelings, the rain returned that night. The next morning, after breakfast, it streamed down the withdrawing room windows until even Fortune turned away. Meredith declared herself ready for a restorative nap and took her pet off with her. Abigail retired to the library.

Finn stood along the wall.

She ought to leave him to the duty he clung to so fiercely. Indeed, there was no sign of the importunate lover today, merely a highly skilled warrior, ready for a battle that might never come.

But it seemed wrong that he should be made to stand while she took her leisure. She should invite him to join her, yet asking him hadn't worked in the past, and she was in no position to issue orders like Roth.

"I am convinced Lord Belfort built sufficiently strong bookcases that we need not fear they will collapse," she tried, turning a page in her book from where she sat on one of the leather-upholstered chairs.

"Lord Belfort did not build these bookcases," he said.

She glanced up. "So, you do suspect their workmanship."

"No. I merely state a fact." Those amber eyes remained fixed on the distance. "Mr. Cowls informed me that Rose Hill has been in Lady Belfort's family for generations. Hence, any workmanship would have been accomplished by someone hired by her or her family."

"Ah." She set the book aside and swiveled to face him

fully, her grey wool skirts brushing the soft carpet at her feet. "Truly, Finn. It's just the two of us. You could sit."

"I have my duty."

Stubborn! "I am sitting, and I can see the door, the window, and even the hearth, should some villain be so inclined to climb down it. Please, sit."

He hesitated.

This could not be entirely about duty. He'd taken her hands last night, danced with her down the line. Remained faithfully at her side.

Like a husband.

All at once, she could imagine an evening in a room such as this, cuddled together on a sofa, reading aloud from some book that kept them both enthralled. What would it matter if the rain poured and the wind blew, so long as they were together?

She set aside her book and rose. "If you will not sit, I will stand."

A frown drew down his brows. "You cannot stand as long as I can."

"Possibly not," she agreed, going to position her back against the bookshelf opposite him. Some of the tomes were wide enough that they jutted out over the edge, pressing against her shoulders. She ignored them. "But a governess must stand about at times too. I'm willing to give it a try."

She regarded him.

He looked through her.

Or, at least, he appeared to be trying to look through her, gaze focused on some spot above her right shoulder. Abigail cocked her head to the right. His gaze veered to center. She straightened and fluttered her lashes. His mouth quirked.

She stuck out her tongue at him.

Finn recoiled. "What was that?"

"A childish display of pique," she admitted. "And a vain attempt to force a laugh."

He chuckled. "Not so vain an attempt."

Encouraged, she pushed away from the bookcase. "Then why won't you sit with me? Meredith will not think less of you. She encourages it as well."

"It could endanger you both," he insisted. "I lost focus before, Abigail. I nearly crippled a man."

Abigail blinked. "What? How?"

He sighed, and the words came out haltingly, as if dragged from his soul. "I thought myself in love once. She was a high-born lady, a daughter to one of King Frederick's courtiers. We were alone in a garden, and I focused more on her than my surroundings. When a sound penetrated, I whirled, blade out, and slashed her brother in the arm. He was a youth, and he had only been coming to check on her, doing his duty where I failed mine. I abandoned my post to rush for the physician. He survived. I am told his arm eventually healed enough to be of use again."

Abigail moved to his side, laying a hand on his. "It wasn't your fault."

"It was." His eyes were hard. "I put my feelings above my duty, and he paid the price."

"And his sister?" she asked, unable to let go of him. "Did she blame you?"

"Her father did," he said. "She cut all ties, at his demand."

Abigail shook her head. "Then she was not in love with you. Love stays, through good times and bad."

His free hand rose, grazed her cheek. "That, I am beginning to believe."

She waited, hoping, heart hammering. His hand fell, and he looked to the chairs. "You should sit. I will join you."

A small victory, at least.

Abigail returned to her seat. Finn came to stand a

moment in front of the chair beside her, looking in all directions, as if to test his vantage point. Then he nudged the chair slightly to the left and sat, resting his hands on the arms.

"Thank you," she murmured. Best to try to be normal after that conversation. "I am reading *The Faerie Queen*. It is an epic poem from the time of chivalry, with gallant knights and resourceful ladies. Do you know it?"

He shook his head. "Read me some of it, if you will."

And so they sat, feet away and miles apart, as she read, and she tried not to think about what the future might hold, without him.

CHAPTER FIFTEEN

BY HALF PAST one, Abigail had convinced herself Preston would not make an appearance after all. She was just as glad. Meredith had returned from her nap, and Finn had consented to join in the conversation, and they had debated everything from the best saddle for riding cross country to the songs one should play at a ball. So when Mr. Cowls announced that Mr. Netherfield had come to call, she stared rather stupidly as Meredith agreed to see him.

Finn went to stand in his customary spot along the wall as Mr. Cowls showed Preston up. Today he was the consummate rising banker, black pin-striped cutaway coat, black trousers, tasteful white waistcoat with an expensive weave. He bowed to Meredith and studiously ignored Finn before offering a bouquet of ruby red chrysanthemums to Abigail, making her wonder whose hothouse he had plundered.

"Their beauty cannot compare to yours, of course," he said with another bow.

Over his back, Meredith raised her brows at Abigail.

"Thank you, Mr. Netherfield," she said. "It was very kind of you. Mr. Cowls, may I trouble you…?"

"No trouble at all, Miss Winchester," the butler said. He took the flowers, cast Preston a considering look, and made his way from the room.

"Won't you sit down, Mr. Netherfield?" Meredith offered.

He sank onto the chair Finn had just vacated. "Thank you, your ladyship. I appreciate your condescension in allowing me to visit. I promise you, I will not abuse your good graces."

"I did not suppose that you would," she said.

Abigail recognized the twitch of her mouth. Meredith was trying hard to take Preston as seriously as he wished, but some part of her wanted to laugh at his pretentious manner.

"Your home is lovely," he commented. "A family estate, I understand."

"Indeed," she said. "And I understand your family resides in London. They are all well, I hope."

"My mother and sisters are quite well," he assured her. "Though they have expressed a desire to see Miss Winchester again."

She glanced at Finn, who also raised a brow. Preston's sisters were dears, but she'd always thought his mother looked at her as if she were a bit of wilted cabbage pretending to be salad.

"I hope you will remember me to them, then," she said.

"You can speak to them directly," he said, "when you return with me to London."

"Oh," Meredith said far too brightly, "had you decided to return to London, my dear?"

Finn was regarding her fixedly.

"No," Abigail said firmly.

"Perhaps not as yet," Preston allowed. "But I have hope I will convince you to see things differently. Perhaps we could take a walk about the estate. The rain had stopped as I climbed out of the coach."

Perhaps a moment together would convince him they had no future. She looked to Meredith. "Would you mind, your ladyship?"

"Not at all," Meredith said before glancing toward the door. "Ah, there you are."

Preston turned, then frowned, clearly expecting to see someone other than a grey-coated cat with copper-colored eyes. Fortune, who had been downstairs, likely inspecting the preparations for dinner and hoping to wheedle a bite, strolled into the room, then crossed to brush against Finn's boots. Next she passed Abigail, head tilted as if soliciting a pet. Finally, she jumped up onto the sofa.

"Fortune," Meredith said, "this is Mr. Netherfield. He came all the way from London to visit Abigail."

Fortune nestled into her lap. Never once did she so much as look at Preston. As if he did not exist.

A laugh bubbled up inside Abigail.

Preston glanced from her to Meredith and back. "I appear to have missed the joke."

"It's all right," Abigail said, swallowing the last of her laughter. She rose. "I'll fetch my pelisse and join you in the entry hall for our walk."

He stood and bowed, and she hurried out. But when she reached the entry hall a short time later, blue pelisse wrapped snuggly about her, she found Finn, Roth, Tanner, and Keller waiting.

Preston did not look amused.

"Surely they need not all accompany us," he said as he and Abigail started on the path along the pond, the four guards at their back.

"I explained that Mr. Huber is my bodyguard," Abigail told him. "The others are likely merely stretching their legs."

"Just so," Tanner called up and proceeded to point a toe at the leaf-strewn ground.

Preston shook his head. "This is nonsense. I am quite capable of protecting you from any harm."

Someone snorted. She thought it was Roth.

She glanced at Preston. She had thought those broad shoulders and long legs the very epitome of a gentleman. But Finn's shoulders appeared to be more muscled, his legs longer and more powerful. His hands were stronger, his movements more confident. He was a poet with a sword. Did Preston even know how to fence?

No, she could not believe him as capable of protecting her.

"Mr. Huber is trained for such things," she explained. "I trust him with my life."

Preston sighed. "I had hoped you would trust *me* with your life."

Likely he meant in marriage. "We have been parted," she said. "On your insistence. You cannot expect me to welcome you back with open arms."

But clearly he expected her to do just that.

"I can see the attraction of this position," he said as they came around the end of the pond, their reflections wavering in the green depths. "The house is impressive, the grounds expansive, and Lady Belfort seems to dote upon you. But, as you noted, she could well release you when her husband returns. And this Society, such as it is, cannot compare to London."

She had enjoyed herself more last night at the assembly than at any ball she'd attended in London. And any dance partner would surely pale in comparison to Finn.

"I rather like Weyton," she said, lifting her skirts around a bump in the path, where tree roots encroached. "It feels like home."

"Your home is in London," he insisted. "Among those who admire you."

Never had anyone looked at her with such admiration as Finn did. And she doubted any employer would be as kind as Meredith. "I am well appreciated here."

"Yet what of our future? We had plans, dreams."

When she thought back, she remembered only

discussing his plans, his dreams. Her father had been his mentor, and Preston had hoped to follow in his footsteps to become a leader at an important bank, making decisions about other people's futures.

Yet he was right about one thing: a good marriage could be preferable to working. Preston might be overly cautious, but that caution offered her security. His presence at her side guaranteed her a place in Society. A governess position offered neither of those things.

Once again, thoughts of Finn intruded. Preston seemed to have changed his mind about the liability she presented to his career. Would the same be said for Finn? Could she follow her heart, with no fear of damaging his chance of advancement?

Did she dare dream of a future with Finn?

How cozy they looked together, walking through the golden autumn light. Abigail's skirts brushed Netherfield's boots, her voice a sweet murmur against his deeper part.

And all Finn wanted to do was punch him in his insufferable smile, shake him until his perfectly combed hair fell about his ears. He wasn't nearly good enough for Abigail.

The others seemed to agree.

"Coward," Roth muttered. "You told us how he left her. How can he pretend to care for her now?"

"He should not be monopolizing her time," Keller agreed with a look to Finn.

"If she favors him, what can I do?" Finn countered.

"Challenge him to a sword fight," Keller suggested as Finn slowed his steps and forced the others to do likewise to give the two a little privacy. "That will show her his weakness."

"And make me look like a tyrant," Finn said. "I doubt he could hold up a sword, much less swing it."

"Challenge him to a duel, then," Roth offered. "Any man might shoot a pistol. Either he runs or you shoot him. That will solve the problem."

And raise a host of others. "Duels are illegal in England," Finn reminded him. "Count Montalban was nearly hanged for the offense."

Roth puffed out a sigh of frustration.

"There's a far simpler way," Tanner put in. "Tell her you love her. I have no doubt she'll choose you."

Roth rounded on him. "He is her bodyguard! He cannot love her."

"He can," Keller put in quietly. "But he cannot act upon it. It would stain his honor."

Though he knew the statement to be true, it stung. "It is not so much a question of love as what is right. She deserves position and wealth, neither of which I can offer her. He can."

Roth's lip curled, but he did not argue. Tanner broke away to stalk toward the house.

"You can protect her," Keller said. "You are good at that."

He was. But there had been no sign of any trouble recently. Was he even needed now?

Or had the trouble truly arrived with Preston Netherfield?

·—————•♡◡·—————·

Meredith could not be sorry for a moment alone. Cowls had brought in the latest mail, and she had fallen upon the beloved handwriting like a starving man a feast.

We have reached Geneva safely, though not without some little adventure. I had never thought to ride out a storm at sea, outrun an avalanche, or fend off brigands.

She lowered the sheet to eye Fortune, who was lounging on a pillow across from her. "I do not know which surprises me more." Shaking her head, she continued reading.

The storm I can reasonably ascribe to Nature, but we have concerns that the avalanche and the brigands might be part of some plan to prevent Batavaria, England, and Württemberg from cementing their alliance. I suspect treachery at every turn. Be careful.

"If he only knew," she told the cat.

Prince Otto Leopold and Larissa send their love. I would send you more than my love—sunshine to caress your face when I cannot, delicacies to touch the lips I long to kiss, friends to gladden the heart that beats in time with mine. Until I can hold you close once more, I remain always, your Julian.

She pressed the letter to her heart, closing her eyes and imagining his warm smile, the feel of his lips against hers.

Fortune must have risen, for Meredith felt her butt her arm. Opening her eyes, she lowered the sheet and ran a hand over her pet's fur.

"Julian is well," she told her. "But we may not be. It seems we may need our guards more than we knew."

———◦♥◦———

Preston would not relent. He attended services on Sunday, sitting piously in the pew across from them. Abigail could almost see the halo over his golden hair. Meredith swept her out of the chapel before he could do more than nod in greeting. The duchess raised a brow as they passed, Julia raised a hand, and Mrs. Bee and her daughters raised a fuss when they failed to grasp a moment of their time.

Still he was undeterred. He called on Monday, and he called on Tuesday. Each time, he had marshaled fresh arguments.

"My mother and sisters will be disappointed," he said on Monday as they sat in the withdrawing room with Meredith and Finn. At least Meredith looked mildly amused by his pleading. Finn looked ready to take out his sword and stab it through the heart of the opposite bookcase. Or Preston.

"I am persuaded they will survive," Abigail said.

Preston edged forward on the chair as if intent on making his case. "But Mother and I were counting on you to be a positive influence. At times, I am convinced that my sisters need schooling in the ways of Society."

As if she knew so much at three years their senior. "They are clever things," Abigail reminded him. "They will learn."

"But who better to teach them?" he pressed. "Is that not why you became a governess, to inspire young ladies?"

"Not ladies of your sisters' ages," she explained. "My charges are generally much younger."

He made the mistake of glancing at Meredith, who rose, forcing him to his feet. "I regret that I have need of Abigail's help this afternoon, aged dame that I am. Thank you for coming, Mr. Netherfield."

"We will disappoint our friends as well," he tried when he returned on Tuesday. This time, Meredith pleaded a headache, though Abigail noticed she retired to the library instead of her bedchamber. And Fortune remained behind.

The cat still continued to pretend Preston didn't exist. She padded between Finn on the wall and Abigail on her chair, seeking attention. Finding insufficient adoration, she wandered to the window and put her back to them all as if finding the view of the birds flitting among the trees far more entertaining.

"Did we have so many friends in common?" Abigail asked her would-be beau. "I do not recall meeting many of yours."

"I was honored to call your father, Mr. Benchley, and the other trustees of the bank acquaintances," he reminded her. "You were well known to them and their wives. Mr. Benchley asks after you on occasion."

"Very kind of him," Abigail said. "But even he knows it best to keep a distance, and the rest have little time for me now. Father's decision saw to that."

He did not argue the point. Likely he knew he couldn't. "The minister at St. Mary's had hoped to marry us. He asked after you just the other day too."

"Tell him I am well and thank him for his concern," Abigail said. "But you have given me no good reason to marry, Preston."

Another man might have taken that opportunity to declare his affection. Preston did not. In fact, not once did he claim he loved her, that she was all he needed in life. He did not rhapsodize about her hair or eyes. He did not extol her virtues. While she did not hope for a sonnet, surely a basic declaration was not too much to expect!

Her gaze drifted to Finn along the wall. No matter how long Preston stayed, those broad shoulders never slumped. An occasional flicker of his golden eyes was all that indicated he was attending to the conversation. But she had no doubt he heard every word.

How would he praise his love? What words would he use to offer his devotion? She had a feeling she wouldn't hear half of them before she threw herself into his arms.

"I begin to think Preston considers me his due," she told Meredith after her former beau had left that day and she had wandered down to the library to check on her employer. Finn had stationed himself near the door, as if expecting to have to defend them from a ravening horde.

"It is his wounded consequence speaking," Meredith said, shuffling through correspondence. "You did not fall into a decline at his defection."

Perhaps. But she only grew more impatient at his requests. She had given him ample opportunities. Time to end this.

He seemed to have come to the same conclusion, for, on Wednesday, he greeted Meredith in the withdrawing room and then planted himself in front of Abigail, arms crossed over his chest. The posture was not nearly as impressive on him as it was on Roth.

"I begin to believe you are dallying with my affections," he declared. "It is unseemly, Abigail. I intend to return to London tomorrow. I urge you to tender your resignation, pack your things, and come with me."

Perhaps it was the militant posture, perhaps the demanding tone in his voice, but Fortune, threading her way past Abigail's skirts, stopped and laid back her ears. With a hiss, she swatted at his boot. He dropped his hands and waved one at her.

"Shoo!"

Meredith rose and scooped her pet up into her arms. "No one tells those I love how to behave in my house, sir. Do not call again. My door is no longer open to you."

He blinked, then snapped a bow. "Your ladyship." Turning, he held out a hand to Abigail. "Come along, then."

Abigail rose, clinging to her composure. "I will go nowhere with you, Mr. Netherfield. I have tried to make my feelings known in the kindest way possible, but you clearly require plain speaking. We have no future together. I agree with Lady Belfort. Do not call again."

"This is your answer?" His eyes widened in shock, and his voice throbbed with hurt. "After all we've been to each other?"

Finn pushed off the wall, forestalling any scold she might have given. "You have overstayed your welcome, Mr. Netherfield." Before Preston could protest, Finn caught him by the collar and began dragging him toward the door.

"Unhand me, you villain!" Preston cried, arms flailing.

Finn obeyed long enough to nudge him toward the stairs. Meredith came to the landing to watch. Abigail joined her, not sure whether to gasp or laugh.

He stumbled down to the entry hall, where Mr. Cowls handed him his hat. It seemed to have acquired a dent along the way. Unheeding, Preston shoved it onto his head and stalked out the door, to where the coach he must have borrowed stood waiting. Keller and Tanner were waiting with it.

"Perhaps more assistance than he required," Meredith mused as the two guardsmen hustled him into the coach and slammed the door.

Keller put his fingers to his mouth and whistled sharply.

The horses bolted down the drive, the carriage swaying alarmingly.

Tanner and Keller shook hands as if well pleased with themselves.

"You are incorrigible!" Abigail called down.

"I will take that as a compliment," Tanner said with a bow.

CHAPTER SIXTEEN

FINALLY. FINN HAD been ready to throw the fellow out the first day he'd called. He'd always admired Abigail's patience and composure, but he couldn't understand why she'd suffered Netherfield as long as she had.

"Someone needs a nice saucer of milk," Lady Belfort said, hand stroking her pet as a low grumbling came from Fortune's throat. "Yes, darling, I know. He was thoroughly tiresome. But we will no longer have to endure his company." She glanced up at Abigail with a smile. "Why don't you see what you can find in the library to amuse you? Fortune and I will be back shortly." Still crooning to the cat, she headed for the stairs.

Abigail followed more slowly, Finn at her side.

"What do you think my chances might be for remaining her companion after her husband returns home?" she asked him as Lady Belfort disappeared down the corridor toward the kitchen.

Was she trying to envision a different future now that she'd ended possibilities with Netherfield? A shame he could not give her hope.

"Lord and Lady Belfort have been present at a number of functions with the prince and king," Finn explained, opening the door to the library for her. A quick glance proved them the only inhabitants. "They are devoted to each other. I cannot imagine her wanting a companion."

"Then perhaps the duchess will require help," she said, going to the far bookshelf and studying its offerings. "As Lady Belfort has mentioned, she must be lonely with her daughters married and off living their lives. Wey Castle would be a very congenial place to reside."

"It is a fine castle," he acknowledged, taking up his place in the corner, where he could see her, the door, and the window. "And Weyfarer House, their townhouse, is fine as well. But I think the duchess and the duke are also devoted to one another. He stays mostly at home. Some call him the Hermit Duke."

She sighed. "Well, I suppose there's always Scotland."

He frowned. "Scotland?"

She pulled down a thick tome. "Yes. I had thought to be as far away from London as possible, to avoid the scandal. But many of the people on the first ship with my father were from Scotland, so perhaps I wouldn't be able to avoid it there, either."

The book wobbled in her grip. He heard the tremor in her voice as well. Despite her evident calm, she still feared the future.

"Perhaps," he said, "you needn't go all the way to Scotland for a new life."

She clutched the book to her chest and turned to stare at him.

Again, he had said too much. A hazard where she was concerned. Those big blue eyes, that trusting smile, made confidences easy.

But he was in no position to offer confidences or anything else.

"Finn?" she asked, gaze searching his.

"A lady of your beauty and talents would be welcome anywhere," he said. Then he started for the door. "Excuse me. I should check the house."

As if there was anything more dangerous here to her than his own longings.

Still, he made a point of taking Lady Belfort aside when she and Fortune returned a short while later.

"It would appear that I am no longer needed as bodyguard," he told her as they stood by the hearth in the library. Abigail was dangling a bit of ribbon to Fortune nearby. "Have you heard anything from this Lord Kendall?"

"No," she admitted, "but never fear, Finn. I will not leave you stranded. Besides, something tells me things are not as settled as they seem. We may have need of your services yet."

Her prediction proved true the very next day.

Finn had hoped they had weathered enough difficult visits, but Mrs. Bee and her daughters came calling again. At the sound of their shrill voices in the entry hall, Fortune darted up to the chamber story and refused to come down. Tanner and Keller had been in the garden, practicing under Roth's critical eye. When Finn sent a footman to warn them, they quickly decamped to the cottage. He wouldn't have been surprised if they had barricaded the door behind them.

Finn stood along the wall, thinking that might deter any conversation. But even his most military stance, feet shoulder width apart, hands clasped behind his back, gaze on the farther wall, did not stop them.

"And how are you today, Mr. Huber?" the oldest asked politely after all the ladies had greeted each other.

"Well," he said.

"He looks well," her sister ventured, being so bold as to glance up and down his person.

"And I trust all of you are well," Abigail put in as if to draw their attention away from him.

The mother fanned herself with one hand. "Far too warm for this time of year, I find. Though it is a good excuse to go driving."

"Do you drive, Mr. Huber?" the youngest put in.

"No," he said.

"But you must!" she protested while her sister looked down at her hands in her lap. "How else are you to travel about the country with your illustrious patrons?"

"Mr. Huber isn't traveling much at the moment," Lady Belfort said. "Are you planning to travel, Miss Bee?"

She pouted. "No, worse luck. Unless, of course, I had a husband to follow."

He refused to meet her gaze.

"I'm sure you'll find a nice Surrey lad to suit you," Lady Belfort said. "The assembly is just the place. How many more are planned before Christmas?"

That, at least, kept them talking for a bit. Finn let the noise wash over him, gaze moving from the window, which showed a blue sky with clouds piling up on the horizon, to the open door, which showed an empty landing.

"Then you intend to stay for some time, Miss Winchester?"

The youngest daughter's question brought his attention back to the lady under his protection. Abigail was seated next to Lady Belfort, a wool shawl draped about her muslin gown.

"As long as Lady Belfort might need me," she said with a smile to her ladyship.

"I do not think I could be a companion," Miss Bee the younger said with a shiver. "Always at the beck and call of another. Always having to be pleasant. Do you have any time to yourself, say to go riding or to come into the village?"

Was she implying Lady Belfort was a harsh mistress? Both her mother and the lady herself seemed to think so, for they were frowning at her. So was her sister.

Abigail answered easily enough. "I could not ask for a kinder patroness. I count myself fortunate indeed to have been invited to stay."

Lady Belfort's frown eased, and she reached out to pat Abigail's hand. "I am the fortunate one to have found you, my dear."

Miss Bee the younger clapped her hands. "Oh, how delightful. Then you will not mind if she comes to visit us, say tomorrow morning?"

Her mother drew herself up. "Do not be ridiculous. Tomorrow morning is entirely inconvenient. And we must not deprive Lady Belfort of her companion." Seemingly satisfied she had silenced her daughter at last, she turned to Lady Belfort. "I do hope we will have the pleasure of your husband's company soon."

"I hope by Christmas," she said, smile tight. "And what are your plans for the season?"

Conversation resumed then, but Miss Angelica Bee continued to watch Abigail, as if searching for any flaw she might exploit. Why? Was she jealous? Abigail was certainly prettier and sweeter natured, but Miss Bee had to know she had little freedom or standing of her own. And why invite her to visit at a specific time? Something more seemed to be brewing behind those sharp blue eyes.

When the footman brought the tea tray, Finn slipped out to meet Mr. Cowls on the landing.

"Ask Mr. Keller to ride escort on the ladies when they leave," he murmured.

The butler raised a snowy brow. "Do you expect mischief?"

"I think mischief may be in the making," Finn explained. "Tell him to wait and see where else they might go after reaching home."

The butler nodded, and Finn returned to his place along the wall.

"These tea cakes are delicious, Lady Belfort," the youngest daughter was gushing. "You must try some, Mr. Huber."

"Yes, Mr. Huber," her sister added. "Please join us."

"Girls," their mother admonished. "You must not tease him. Leave the man to his duty."

Now both daughters pouted.

It seemed the mother at least had finally realized he and his comrades were not the best matches for her daughters. He was only thankful they ended their visit a short time later. He watched with Abigail from the landing as the butler saw them out. The daughters still squealed in delight when Keller rode up to accompany them.

Abigail bumped his shoulder. "Why sacrifice Keller to their machinations? Surely you aren't still worried about the mythical highwaymen."

"I am more interested in who else they might meet on the road," Finn told her.

She cocked her head. "And who else do you suspect?"

"Keller will report soon enough," Finn promised her. "Perhaps you should go tell Fortune it is safe to come down."

With a laugh, she lifted her skirts and started up the stairs.

Keller came back as the sun was setting and asked for a word with Finn. Lady Belfort and Abigail were upstairs changing for dinner, so he stepped out onto the drive with the younger guardsman. The breeze nipped at his cheeks, promising colder days ahead.

"What did you learn?" Finn asked.

"Mrs. Bee and her daughters returned to their home a little outside the village," he reported, rubbing his freshly shaved chin with the back of one hand. "After about a half hour, the two daughters and a maid walked out and down to the linen drapers. I left the horse at the blacksmith's and followed."

"Did they meet anyone?" Finn pressed.

"Not at first," Keller qualified. "They seemed determined to examine the fellow's wares. I have never understood how women can spend so much time shopping. Need a ribbon, find a ribbon, pay for it, go home. Why look over every ribbon in the store?"

"There is an art to it," Finn assured him, remembering the times he had accompanied Lady Giselle shopping. "What is the quality of the ribbon? Does it match or compliment the gown? Can it be used to trim more than one? Will it enhance her coloring, draw attention to her eyes? Is there a better bargain to be had here or at another shop?"

Keller's brows shot up. "I had no idea the matter was so complicated. That would explain why they stayed for more than an hour. I thought it was only because they were waiting for someone."

Finn stilled. "Who?"

Keller met his gaze. "Mr. Netherfield. They spoke for some time before the ladies left him. The older daughter did not look amused. The younger did most of the talking. I followed Netherfield to the inn, where he appears to be staying."

He was supposed to have left for London today. Had he stayed for some other reason? How did he know the Bees?

And had he found another way to spy on Abigail, through them?

―――◦⚬♥⚬◦―――

Finn had been restive all afternoon. Abigail wasn't sure why. A visit from the Bees was never particularly pleasant, but Meredith seemed compelled to receive them, likely because of their standing in the area. Still, even she pushed her prawns about her plate that night, and Finn did not appear interested in any of the choice food.

Abigail glanced between the two thoughtful faces.

Below the table, Fortune bumped her leg, as if encouraging her to speak.

"Is something wrong?" Abigail ventured.

Meredith set down her fork. "In all the bustle, I forgot to tell you. My Julian wrote at last."

"Oh, marvelous!" Abigail exclaimed even as Finn perked up. "That is, assuming he is well and safe."

"At the moment," she said. "But he writes that they have been plagued by mishaps, and he begins to suspect not all were accidents. He is concerned the enemies of Batavaria may be trying to hinder the ratification of the agreement."

Finn's face hardened. "Then the spy may have been after us all along."

Part of her was relieved not to be the cause of more distress, yet the injustice of having Finn spied upon rankled. Like her, the four Imperial Guards found themselves embroiled in trouble not of their making.

"Very possible," Meredith said. "Although it is also possible the fellow had something to do with Abigail's father and the Poyais scandal."

The candlelight seemed to dim.

"Or Preston Netherfield," Finn said. "I find myself glad that you threw him out."

"Actually, you threw him out," Abigail reminded him. "I just asked him to leave."

Finn shoved back his plate, and the footman came to remove it. "It appears he has not left. He met with the two Misses Bee today in Weyton."

Abigail frowned. So did Meredith.

"How do you know?" her patroness asked.

"I asked Keller to watch them." He sounded completely unrepentant about the matter.

"I never knew where he was staying," Abigail mused. "Could he be acquainted with the Bees?"

"If they had known you had acquaintances in common,

they would have been swift to claim it," he pointed out. "Beginning with the night of the assembly. Besides, Keller says they met at the linen drapers. They would not have had to resort to such subterfuge if he had been staying with them."

"True," Abigail allowed. She rubbed her hands on her napkin. "And I'm surprised he would choose to linger in any regard. His stated reason for being in Weyton was to importune me to return with him. Failing that, why remain?"

"Perhaps he hopes to persuade you yet," Finn said, watching her.

Abigail dropped the napkin. "Well, he hopes in vain."

He raised a brow. "You are certain?"

"Absolutely! He cannot hold a candle…" She stopped and drew in a breath before the truth spilled out. Now Meredith raised a brow as well.

"He cannot hold my affections," Abigail finished. "But if you are concerned that he remains in Weyton, perhaps we should discover his reasoning."

He shook his head. "There is no *we*. I am your bodyguard. It is my duty to protect you."

Abigail shook her head at his vehemence. "Preston knows about the scandal. It is the very reason he broke things off. He has no reason to wish me harm. I say we beard the lion in his den and order him to move along."

"I say we allow Finn to beard the lion," Meredith countered, "while we take on the lioness and her cubs. I would be very interested to hear how Mrs. Bee's daughters came to the attention of Mr. Netherfield."

Finn's jaw tightened. "Take Keller with you, then."

Meredith tsked. "Taking any of you with us will only force Miss Bee the younger to continue her flirting."

"We need her to talk about more important matters," Abigail agreed. "I'm not concerned about them, Finn. I am quite immune to their feeble stings after what happened with my father. And any true villain would surely be sure to give Mrs. Bee wide berth."

He inclined his head. Surrendering, for now.

He seemed no more pleased with the matter the next morning, but he accompanied them inside the coach into the village. A few ladies were out, shopping baskets over their arms and shawls tucked close against the biting breeze. Leaves swirled down the cobblestones to dance against the white cottages. Meredith's coachman let him off at the inn.

"You will be careful," he ordered, hand on the door.

"Always," Meredith assured him.

With a last frown, he shut the door and stepped back.

He was protecting her. It was his duty.

But suddenly Abigail wanted more, as dangerous as that might be. The words he used, the touch of his hand, the warmth in his eyes, promised her that he saw her as more than just a duty. Her very presence seemed to encourage him to take chances, to trust again.

Could she help him see her as a wife?

CHAPTER SEVENTEEN

FINN STRODE THROUGH the inn yard, trying hard not to look back more than once. He could not like leaving Abigail, but he had to trust she could take care of herself in this situation. Surely she and Lady Belfort were a match for the Bees. He needed to run Preston Netherfield to ground.

"Ah, one of our Imperial Guards," the innkeeper heralded as Finn ducked into the inn. "How might I help you, good sir?"

Finn glanced around the room. No customers were in evidence. Nevertheless, he leaned on the scarred counter. "I seek one of your guests. Mr. Netherfield, of London."

"Popular fellow," he said, leaning on the counter as well. "You're the second to come seeking him today."

Finn did not let his interest show. "And who else would that be?"

"Another stranger," he supplied with a shrug. "Not that you and your friends are strangers any longer. Weyton's own army, eh?" He chuckled at the idea.

Finn allowed himself a smile. "Why would two strangers come to Weyton?"

"Mr. Netherfield claimed he had acquaintances in the area, though none came here to join him," he volunteered. "The other fellow has wandered in for a pint now and again over the last fortnight, but he isn't staying with us." He shook his head at such foolishness.

"Short older fellow," Finn guessed, "eyes perhaps too small for his face."

The innkeeper slapped his hand down on the counter. "The very one. Friend of yours?"

"No," Finn assured him. "Did you get their direction?"

"They left an hour ago, and I haven't seen them since. Shall I take a message?" His eyes were bright with anticipation.

"I'll find Netherfield myself," Finn said. "But thank you."

Outside, he hesitated. The village wasn't large, but he could hardly go door to door, demanding to know if Preston Netherfield and a squinty-eyed man had come to call.

Abigail's former beau had won this hand, but Finn would not give up the game until he knew she was safe.

———•♥•———

The family Bee lived just beyond the village, in a fine building of creamy stone with an impressive pediment over the door. However, the drive was lined with black marble urns as tall as a horse, and banners flew from every window, as if a king had come to visit. Inside, each wall was covered with massive paintings framed in gilt, until she could not be sure of the wallpaper, and every piece of furniture was gilded or tasseled or both.

"Lady Belfort!" Mrs. Bee cried, coming down the curving rosewood stair with one hand held out in entreaty. Her youngest daughter followed at a similar rapid clip, descending on them in the marble-tiled entry hall. The older Miss Bee came more slowly, smile pleased and gaze curious. The cloud of rose-scented perfume was so thick Abigail could almost see it.

"I do believe this is the first time you have visited," Mrs. Bee said, smiling like a cat in the cream. She led them to a withdrawing room off the entry hall. "You must make yourself at home."

That would have been impossible. The room was long and high, but every inch was filled with sofas, credenzas, and more of the urns, these gold. The black-lacquered pianoforte huddled in the corner as if trying to defend itself from the clutter.

In the end, Meredith took possession of one of the sofas, Mrs. Bee took possession of Meredith, and Abigail managed to find a chair nearby before the daughters did. They elected to sit on a flanking sofa.

"Forgive the sudden intrusion," Meredith said. "But I recently learned we have an acquaintance in common."

Mrs. Bee patted her curls. "I cannot be shocked. Good people generally know other good people, I find."

Meredith's smile was tight. "Precisely. Which is why I was surprised to learn that you know Preston Netherfield."

Mrs. Bee frowned. Her older daughter, however, paled and sent her sister a look.

The youngest brightened. "You remember, Mama. The London gentleman who was so attentive at the assembly."

Mrs. Bee's brow cleared. "Ah, yes. Presentable enough fellow. Banker, I believe."

"But you only met at the assembly?" Abigail put in.

Mrs. Bee regarded her as if wondering why one of her urns would elect to speak. "Yes. He claimed to have had dealings with Mr. Bee."

Meredith sighed. "So like him. Encroaching, Mrs. Bee. You may count on it. More likely to ask for a favor than to grant one."

The younger daughter squirmed in her seat. It seemed Abigail hadn't been the only one to be taken in by a ready address.

Meredith leaned closer, as if about to impart a secret, and Mrs. Bee's eyes widened.

"A word of advice," Meredith murmured. "I have

found him to be inconstant. You would not want him for your girls."

Mrs. Bee raised both her chins. "Certainly not." She glared at her daughters. "They have had no contact with Mr. Netherfield since the assembly."

The youngest studied her hands in the lap of her fine kerseymere gown. Her sister cringed. "Actually, Mama, we saw him at the linen draper's yesterday. I had the impression he had expected us to be there." She looked to her sister.

Miss Bee the younger raised her head in a look entirely like her mother's. "He asked me to meet him. He wanted to speak about friends in the area."

He'd wanted to speak about Abigail. Finn had been right. Preston was spying on her, using the younger Miss Bee as his eyes and ears.

"Your beauty is a curse," her mother said with a shake of her head, before looking to Meredith. "Every gentleman is drawn to her. I have to be careful, I can tell you."

"It is the job of every mother," Meredith agreed.

Mrs. Bee frowned at her youngest. "But there will be no more of that, young lady. From now on, if you leave the house, I'll be coming with you."

Miss Bee the younger glared at Abigail, as if this was all her fault. Miss Bee the elder's shoulders relaxed.

Abigail smiled politely. Funny how composure was easy when she couldn't care what the other person thought of her.

Meredith managed to extricate them from the house in quick order then, though Mrs. Bee insisted on following them all the way to the door.

"We must see more of each other," she warbled as they crossed the entry hall. "We have so much in common."

"Should opportunities arise," Meredith said before escaping.

"Masterful," Abigail said when they were safely back in the coach and headed into the village.

Meredith gave her a small smile. "One learns. A part of me would like to pretend she doesn't exist, as Fortune did with Mr. Netherfield, but Julian and her husband have had dealings. I should not like to alienate Mr. Bee."

"The illusive Mr. Bee," Abigail said with a laugh. "I would like to meet the fellow who can survive such a family!"

"I will make a point of introducing you at the next assembly," Meredith promised. "Provided the man makes an appearance."

"Then you expect me to be in residence in the next month," Abigail hazarded.

Meredith smiled. "You may stay as long as you like, but I have a feeling a great many things will change shortly."

She began to hope as well.

Finn was pacing up and down in front of the linen draper's when they came back through the village. He had the door open the moment the coach came to a halt. His narrowed gaze swept the interior, as if he thought to find the highwaymen holding Meredith and Abigail hostage. She almost expected him to bark "report" like Roth.

Instead, Meredith spoke first as he was climbing in. "What news of our so-called friend?"

"He appears to have found a friend of his own," he replied. "It may be our spy with the squinty eyes."

Abigail stared at him. "Preston hired him too? How dare he!"

"And his purpose now?" Meredith asked with a frown.

Finn shook his head. "Unknown. What did you learn from the Bees?"

"Only that Preston introduced himself at the assembly and sought to manipulate the daughters into giving him more information," Abigail told him. "Mrs. Bee was not pleased."

Finn narrowed his eyes. "Then I will be on watch until we know Preston Netherfield has left Weyton for good."

She could only take comfort in that. Bad enough that Preston had convinced Miss Bee to carry tales. How could he have hired someone to spy on her! He knew she was innocent of any crime. And if he had been so concerned for her safety, he could have come sooner and stayed by her side, like Finn.

It was clear he liked the revelations no better than she did, for he did not leave her all afternoon. Yet as her indignation cooled, her daring idea from earlier popped into her mind again.

Could she help Finn see her as a candidate for his wife?

She was certainly a better candidate than the daughters Bee. She would not expect him to cavort with royalty or be an ornament for her arm. But it felt like forever since she had attempted to catch a gentleman's eye. She remembered dressing carefully, but all her prettiest gowns had been sold. Her only jewels were a small strand of her mother's pearls.

But surely courting was more than dressing and flirting. It was finding commonalities like an appreciation for poetry and a devotion to duty. It was an understanding of what it meant to lose family and find another. It was seeing the world through complementary frames, crafting friendship, trust. She and Finn already had that foundation. She just had to build upon it.

She came down to dinner with her head held high and her heart full of hope. The maid had dressed her hair in braided loops, Meredith's pink ballgown draped her curves, her mother's pearls hugged her neck, and a white shawl embroidered with roses covered her shoulders. She knew Finn noticed her finery, for his gaze lingered on her as she joined him and Meredith in the Great Hall.

Her shawl slipped. He caught it and slid it back into place, his hand grazing the tender flesh of her neck. She found herself captured by the glow in his eyes.

And she'd thought to attract *him*!

He offered her his arm, and she allowed him to escort her in to dinner. Meredith smiled a knowing smile as she took her place at the head of the table.

Finn watched her as she ate. She should be used to it by now. Yet she found herself fascinated by the sweep of dark lashes against his cheeks, the curve of his mouth in a smile. She should think of something to say, but she found herself strangely tongue-tied.

Meredith had no such trouble. "Keller was telling me that you enjoy poetry, Finn," she said. "What drew you to it?"

Abigail hurriedly swallowed her mouthful of roast to hear the answer better.

"There is a power to it," he mused, slicing off a bit of beef. "The language, the meter of it spoke to me. Often, it conveys thoughts I cannot put into words."

"Just so," Abigail said. "And in a language so compelling it is impossible to ignore."

He nodded. "Do you have a favorite poet?"

She smiled. "Too many to count, I fear. Blake, Wordsworth, Marvell."

"Writers for the ages," Meredith agreed. "And you, Finn? Who do you favor?"

"You likely would not know her," he said. "She earned the title of Poet Laureate to the King in Batavaria before the war with Napoleon, but she passed away before our victory was secured. Madame Ursula LeBrun Hofer."

A lady poet. How wonderful. "What do you like about her writing?" Abigail asked.

"She understood the soul of Batavaria," he said. "She wrote of the mountains—how they shelter us, offer us food and wood for the fire, yet can cause such devastation. Every Batavarian could appreciate the feeling."

With his family lost in an avalanche, he certainly could.

"We will have to see if we can order a copy of her works when next we're in London," Meredith said.

As dinner ended, Abigail knew he would leave. Tonight was Tanner's evening to stay with them, but she doubted she would take any comfort in his smiling face. As it was, she clung to Finn's arm as he escorted her out of the dining room. Meredith went ahead of them, Fortune passing with an arch look.

Abigail must have been sufficiently hesitant, for he stopped in the middle of the Great Hall. The fire had been banked, and only a few candles remained lit, giving the place a soft glow.

"Must you go?" she murmured.

"It is time," he said. "Unless you have a reason you wish me to stay."

A dozen reasons, a hundred! "I am coming to care for you," she blurted out.

He stilled.

Oh, what had she done! Where was composure, subtlety?

"Forgive me," she hurried on. "I had no right. I know you have your duty, your plans for the future. It's simply that I…"

He swept her into his arms and kissed her.

Warmth, joy, a security she had missed for so long—they tumbled through her until she couldn't untangle one from the other. She clung to him, gave him back his kiss, accepted another. How had she ever considered anything but being at his side?

At last he drew back, but only a little, as if he too was loathe to part. "I care for you too," he murmured, resting his forehead against hers. "Enough to know that you could do better."

She shook her head, skin pressed to his. "Never. But I fear the same for you. What if this scandal doesn't ease? What if associating with me stains you as well?"

He straightened and brought her hand to his lips for a kiss that made her knees tremble. "Perhaps we can worry about that tomorrow. For now, I must be a gentleman and leave you."

With a bow, he did just that.

CHAPTER EIGHTEEN

Abigail had no idea how she managed to sleep that night. Finn cared about her! He cared! There was a chance for a future, if only they could find their way, together.

As it was, she floated down the stairs the next morning for breakfast. Normally, Finn would have joined them afterward, but she found him already in the dining room, as if he couldn't wait to meet again either. Every mouthful, she was smiling.

He smiled back.

"What a lovely morning," Meredith said, applying herself to her kippers and eggs. "Perhaps a walk in the garden after breakfast?"

"Delighted," Abigail said.

With Fortune on her benighted leash, they wandered the paths, where leaves trickled down in the sunlight and seedpods rattled in the breeze. Finn walked beside her, reaching down to cup her fingers and sending a little thrill through her. He even sat beside her when they returned to the library. Fortune brushed between them, as if offering them a blessing.

"Mail, your ladyship," Mr. Cowls said, delivering the pile of letters that had just been brought in from the village.

At the desk, Meredith perked up and began to sort through them.

Finn's hand dangled down the side of the chair, close enough that Abigail could tickle the back with her fingers. His mouth twitched.

"And for you, Miss Winchester," the butler said, offering her a missive.

Finn straightened, and his hand fell away.

"Me?" Abigail took it with a frown. "Thank you, Mr. Cowls, but who would write to me here?"

"You will only know if you open it," Meredith teased before bending over her own pile again.

Abigail did not recognize the handwriting, but she broke the seal and unfolded the note.

My dear girl, forgive me for not contacting you sooner. I had hoped not to trouble you with that sorry business about Poyais again.

Oh, why now! She glanced to the bottom of the note to determine the sender, then drew in a breath. "It is from Mr. Benchley, my father's friend at the bank."

"Good news, I hope?" Meredith asked.

"We shall see." Conscious of Finn's gaze on her, Abigail kept reading.

I learned your direction from Mr. Netherfield. I do hope you have found it in you to accept his abject apologies. He has become something of a watering pot, bemoaning his mistake in letting you go.

She snorted, and Meredith raised a brow. Finn leaned closer.

Regardless, some news has reached me that I do not wish to put into print. I was traveling through Surrey and thought to speak with you directly. Given our association with that horrid scandal, I would not want to impose myself on your benefactress. Yet the news is such that it could have dire consequences if not addressed immediately.

She swallowed in a throat gone tight. News? What news? Did the bank intend to press charges? Or had the other investors succeeded in getting the government to punish those associated with the scheme? She pulled her shawl closer against a growing chill.

I will attempt to stop at the village church in Weyton at one on Saturday. I pray you will remember the affection that once passed between our families and meet me there. If you cannot, I will understand. Regardless, I remain your dear friend always, Cornelius Benchley.

"You are pale," Finn said as she raised her head.

"Very likely," she told him. She looked to her patroness. "Meredith, might I have the afternoon off and the use of the coach?"

Meredith regarded her. "May I ask why?"

"Mr. Benchley will be in the area and wishes to meet me in Weyton. Something to do with Poyais, which is why he would prefer not to bring you into the matter."

"Very well," she allowed. "But you will take Finn with you?"

"I will insist on it," he warned her.

"And I would have it no other way," Abigail assured him.

Yet the lovely autumn day had darkened with her mood. The letter was proof that she might never be free of her father's transgression.

Finn couldn't like it. A letter, out of nowhere, inviting her to meet alone? That promised trouble. Accordingly, he sent a footman to the cottage to alert Roth and the others. They were waiting on the drive when he escorted Abigail to the carriage at half past twelve.

"I seem to require an army," she said with a look to him.

"Merely outriders for the queen," Tanner told her, holding open the door.

Roth rolled his eyes, but once she was safely inside, he

and the others bent closer to Finn to plan their attack. Finn informed the coachman, who nodded agreement. Then Roth climbed up beside the coachman, and Finn, Tanner, and Keller climbed in with Abigail.

"It may be nothing, truly," she said as the coach set out for the village. "Mr. Benchley and my father were good friends. He has been tarred by the same brush. He has no reason to harm me."

"You assume the letter is actually from Benchley," Finn said.

"I did wonder," she said in the gentle tone he had heard her use with her students. "But who else would know the details? Mr. Netherfield, certainly, but we know he is here in Weyton. The letter bore a postmark from London."

"That does not mean it is innocent," Finn insisted.

"Then I will be all the more glad for your escort," she said with a smile that included Tanner and Keller.

By the tightness in their shoulders and the angles of their gazes, Finn knew his friends were just as watchful as the coach approached the village, then rolled to a stop where a copse of trees shadowed the lane.

Abigail glanced among them. "We haven't reached the church. Why are we stopping here?"

"A preventive measure only," Tanner assured her. With a nod to Finn, he and Keller climbed down. Roth joined them, and the three loped into the woods.

"They will meet us at the church," Finn promised her as the coach set out once more.

"You are taking no chances," she commented.

"None," he told her. "We guard something too precious to lose."

Her cheeks turned pink.

After their kiss last night, he had only wanted to gather her close once more. By word and deed, she had won his heart. He'd imagined a position, a home, her at his side.

Now he couldn't afford such a distraction, not when her life might be in danger. Duty must be all.

When they reached the church, Finn helped Abigail out onto the grass. Inside the wrought iron fence, the gravestones were low enough that they would have been hard to hide behind, but there were trees along the edge that might provide cover. He could only hope his comrades were already nestled among them, watching.

His gaze came back to Abigail, waiting patiently beside him. Trusting that he would protect. And he would, always.

"I will go into the church first," Finn told her. "Wait here until I call for you."

As he started forward, she grabbed his hand. "Please, Finn. Be careful. You are precious too, you know."

He brought her hand to his lips for a kiss, savoring the little shiver that went through her at his touch. Then he released her and went through the gate.

He saw nothing moving in the churchyard as he crossed it. Yet everything had a brightness to it, as if he could make out each detail, anything that could be a danger to her—the tilt to the roof's edge that might signal a loose tile, the shadow of the recessed doorway, where a villain might lurk. When he had squired Lady Giselle, he had lost track of the location, the time. Now, he felt every second.

Abigail was the air he breathed, the song that rang in his heart. Despite all his efforts, she had become a part of him.

The main door of the church swung open silently, and he slipped into the little vestibule, noting the light filtering in blue and red and green from the stained glass windows, the musty scent of incense and beeswax, the stillness.

The click of a pistol cocking.

"Do not move, Mr. Huber," Preston Netherfield said,

stepping closer. "I should hate to mar the church floor with blood."

———•○♥○•———

Abigail waited beside the coach, head cocked as she watched the door of the church. Very likely Finn was checking every pew, the altar, and the loft, the dear man. All to ensure she was safe. How had she earned such devotion, such love? How could she ever thank him for it?

A man strode from around the church, greatcoat flapping. She blinked, sure she must have mistaken him.

"Here now!" the coachman called.

Whirling, she found two men clambering up onto the coach. In a moment, they'd taken the reins and driven the vehicle out of sight around the side of the church.

Leaving her alone, with Lord Granbury.

He stopped within a few feet of her. Under the shade of his top hat, his skin looked pale.

"Miss Winchester," he said. "You have put me to some trouble."

Composure, she told her racing heart. Finn would return any moment. Granbury might think her alone and a victim, but she was done with that.

"I'm terribly sorry, my lord," she said politely. "I had thought I made it clear that I no longer wish to be your daughters' governess."

"A shame," he said, "for I would have been able to keep a close eye on you that way. Instead, I find myself in the position of having to offer you a pact. I will write a glowing letter of recommendation for your services, saying nothing about your unfortunate involvement with the Poyais scheme, and you will swear in writing to say nothing of my involvement."

The pieces slotted into place. "You were involved in

the scheme? But, of course you were. So many invested. You thought to profit as well."

"Profit." He spit out the word. "I was promised an estate! A dukedom! My family would have had the honor and position denied them by fickle royalty here. Instead, I would be the laughingstock of London should my involvement become known. I have worked too hard for my reputation to see it brought so low."

"And you would rely on my word never to tell another?" she pressed, trying not to look at the door of the church for Finn.

"I believe that may be sufficient," he said. "Netherfield tells me you are not the type to resort to blackmail. That seems more his style, but so long as I patronize his bank, he will be content. He has been a useful tool, so focused on his own needs he conveniently ignores strictures that might daunt more scrupulous men. And I can always destroy you both if you betray me."

She did not doubt him. He was too wedded to position to allow it to slip through his fingers. But neither she nor Preston would ever be safe so long as he was free to do as he pleased.

"You must give me time to consider," she said, trying to keep him in place until Finn returned. Surely he had heard the coach drive off. And what of Meredith's coachman? Would those villains harm him too?

"Don't be ridiculous," he said. "I am doing this to protect us both."

Abigail shook her head. "This isn't protection. I am well acquainted with it now. And it is standing right behind you."

He jerked about.

She shoved any pretense of composure aside and scrambled back from him.

"Help!" she screamed. "Tanner! Keller! Roth! Finn and I are in danger!"

A guard sprang from the trees, another popped up from behind a headstone, and the third materialized from around the church. In moments, Lord Granbury was surrounded.

Abigail held up her hand to keep them from pouncing on the fellow. "Where is Mr. Huber?" she demanded.

"Here." Finn came from the church, dragging Preston, who stumbled along beside him. He tossed her one-time beau at Lord Granbury's feet and moved in beside her.

"Is this our villain?" he asked with a nod to his lordship.

"Apparently so," Abigail said, drawing a deep breath now that she knew him to be safe. "With Mr. Netherfield's help, it seems."

"This is your father's fault," Preston complained, pausing to spit blood from a split lip. He struggled to his feet. "His decisions landed us all in this predicament."

"Be silent," Lord Granbury warned him before looking to Roth, who he must have taken for their leader. "I am a peer of the realm, sirrah. You have no right to detain me."

"We may not," Finn answered even as Roth glowered. "But I know someone who has."

Abigail wasn't certain the Duke of Wey would agree to see them under such circumstances, but it seemed the legend of the Imperial Guards still held strong, for they were ushered into his presence within minutes of knocking at the castle door.

While Tanner had taken charge of Preston and Lord Granbury, Roth and Keller had rounded up his lordship's servants, who had captured Meredith's coachman. Abigail had paid scant attention to the proceedings. She had been more concerned for Finn.

"Did he dare to strike you?" she demanded, reaching

up a hand to his forehead and checking for any mark on that fine skin.

"Give me some credit," he said with a smile. "He attempted to hold me at bay with a pistol while Lord Granbury spoke with you. It didn't take long to disarm him. What took longer was to convince him to tell me why they were there." He directed a scowl to where Tanner was stuffing Lord Granbury unceremoniously into his coach. "Netherfield did indeed start to seek you, fearing you might tell someone about his involvement in the matter."

Abigail let her hand drop. "Then he never wanted to marry me."

"Oh, he wanted to marry you," Finn said, tone darkening. "He thought a wife would be less likely to tell tales on her husband. But in his searching, he made the acquaintance of Lord Granbury, who urged him to return you to London. When you refused to have anything do with Netherfield, he appealed to his lordship, who sent word to his spy that he would be coming himself."

"Then that fellow who warned me in London and tumbled out of the tree here worked for Lord Granbury, not Preston," Abigail said with a shake of her head.

"So I understood. As did the Bow Street Runner, who traced you from your lodging house to Surrey. Granbury himself wrote the letter that led you here. But Granbury and Netherfield are so used to lying, I'm not sure either of them is telling the truth, about anything. His Grace the Duke of Wey may be able to get to the heart of the matter."

So, Tanner had driven Lord Granbury's carriage, with Roth inside to ensure his lordship and Preston behaved and Keller on the roof to keep the servants in line, while Abigail and Finn followed in Meredith's coach.

"And you're certain you're all right?" Abigail had begged as the coach rattled over the bridge spanning the duke's canal, which separated the village from the island on which his castle lay. "When you didn't come out, I worried."

"And you will never know the fear that speared me when I heard you scream," he said. He shifted across the coach to put himself at her side. "You are all I think about, Abigail. You make me want to climb mountains, cross rivers, face wolves and bears so long as it keeps me at your side."

"Oh, Finn," she said. She had to touch him again, fingers catching on the beginning of stubble as she caressed his cheek. "I feel the same way. But I was right. Too many know of my father's involvement in the Poyais scheme. Will I ever be free of it? Will it brand us, our children?"

A grin spread across his face. "Children. I like the sound of that. A girl with your cleverness. A boy to take up my name."

She laughed. "The last time I checked, sir, only God can determine whether we have sons or daughters."

"Either," he said. "Both. I will love them all the same. Just as I love you."

She fell into his arms, then, and she was only recalled to the present when a footman for the duke opened the coach door and gaped.

Hurriedly drawing on her composure, she descended on Finn's arm to find the other Imperial Guards with their prisoners. And thus they made their way to the duke's library.

She had envied his children such a space when she'd been in residence. Bookcases crowded every side, from floor to high ceiling, with some jutting out at right angles. She would have been happy to travel through that maze of literature. In the center stood a teak desk with curved legs, faced by padded leather chairs.

Behind the desk, brown hair warm and jade eyes cool,

His Grace the Duke of Wey sat gazing at them as if wondering which to hang from the castle wall first.

His words, however, were welcoming.

"Mr. Huber," he said with a nod. "Mr. Roth, Mr. Keller, Mr. Tanner, always good to see you. And Miss Winchester. I had not thought to meet again, especially under such circumstances."

Now Preston was gaping as badly as the footman, and Lord Granbury was turning paler with each word. Apparently, they had thought her utterly friendless. Thank God for Meredith, the Imperial Guards, and Finn.

She offered the duke her best smile and dipped a curtsey. "Your Grace. Thank you for receiving us."

"Indeed." He leaned back in his seat as she straightened. "Who intends to explain why you've come to my door, in my role as magistrate?"

Lord Granbury shook off Tanner's grip and pushed forward. "This is an outrage. I am Granbury, a peer of the realm, like yourself. I have been accosted, ordered about, and inconvenienced by these louts. I demand that you lock them up immediately."

"Interesting," the duke said, lower lip out. He turned to Roth. "And your side of the matter, Mr. Roth?"

Roth looked to Finn. "Huber will explain."

Finn stepped forward. "These two men, Lord Granbury and the banker Preston Netherfield, both of London, followed Miss Winchester to Rose Hill, threatened and harassed her, and appeared to be about to attempt kidnapping, had we not been there to stop them."

Oh, but he was magnificent! Those flashing eyes, that proud tilt of his head, his aura of command. Surely the duke would be as impressed!

Lord Granbury, however, began blustering again. "Lies! Slander!"

The duke held up his hand to silence him, then turned to Abigail. "Are you pressing charges, Miss Winchester?"

They all looked to her.

Perhaps she should. A part of her would greatly enjoy seeing Preston's so vaulted reputation torn to shreds. And Lord Granbury could use a lesson in how to treat people.

But punishing them would not solve the problem.

She shook her head. "No, Your Grace."

CHAPTER NINETEEN

FINN WAS STARING at her. So were the other guards. Lord Granbury's smile turned up, knowing. She would not give him the satisfaction of thinking she intended to agree to his demand for a pact between them.

"Lord Granbury and Mr. Netherfield were the victims of a cruel hoax you may have read about in the newspapers," she said, and his lordship's smile fled. "The madness concerning Colonel MacGregor and the so-called country of Poyais infected far too many and led to too much hardship. These men did not want their involvement known. I knew of it, and so they sought to silence me, by whatever means necessary. By telling you, I put an end to their predations."

The Duke of Wey smiled, and Abigail knew he understood. Now, if only she could convince Finn.

"A wise move indeed," the duke said. "But I would expect no less from the governess who so ably managed her schoolroom despite the age differences, skills, and interests of her students." His gaze swiveled to land on Lord Granbury and Preston, and his face hardened.

Lord Granbury's gaze skittered away. Preston cringed.

"Miss Winchester will not be pressing charges," the duke said. "But that does not prevent me from holding you over to the Assizes for judgment."

Lord Granbury rallied. "Now, see here," he started.

"I see more than you might like, Granbury," the duke

said. "I have been involved in discussions in Parliament about these heinous proceedings concerning Poyais. That you were associated and attempted to hide the fact rather than help other victims puts a question on your intelligence and your character. You will have nothing further to do with Miss Winchester, or I will bring you up on charges myself. Mr. Netherfield?"

Preston looked up shakily. "Your Grace?"

"I am unfamiliar with your involvement. Enlighten me."

Preston glanced at Abigail, then dropped his gaze once again. "Colonel MacGregor approached the bank where I and Miss Winchester's father worked about a loan. When Mr. Winchester was debating recommending the investment, I encouraged him to take the risk."

Abigail pressed her hand to her lips. "Oh, Preston, you didn't."

"It looked sound!" He spoke more to the duke than to her. "I thought my career made. How was I to know MacGregor was a charlatan? It was all I could do to distance myself for my family's sake."

"And you were willing to harm Miss Winchester rather than have your involvement known." The duke's eyes narrowed to slits of green. "If I learn you have come within ten feet of her again, for any purpose, I will advise your superiors at your bank that you are untrustworthy and should be discharged immediately. For now, I want you out of Surrey by nightfall. Good day, sir."

Preston managed a bow. "Your Grace." Without even glancing at Abigail, he fled.

Lord Granbury stood a moment, chin up. Then he turned and stalked out of the library, his staff trailing after him.

"Gentlemen," the duke said, looking to Finn and the other guards. "Is there anything else you need of me?"

Roth, Keller, and Tanner glanced at Finn.

"No, Your Grace," he said. "Thank you."

"That decision could only be called the wisdom of Solomon," Tanner agreed.

The tilt of His Grace's mouth suggested a smile. "Be glad there were no babies to cleave in two today, Mr. Tanner. Miss Winchester, I wish you the best of luck. I only regret there are no children currently in my schoolroom or you can be sure I would be making further use of your talents."

Abigail curtsied again. "Thank you, Your Grace." The guards followed her out.

"I'll tell the coachman," Keller offered before ranging ahead down the corridor.

"I'll make sure the others have gone," Roth said, moving after him.

"I can think of nothing that needs doing," Tanner admitted with a grin. "But I know when I'm not wanted." He too headed for the door.

Abigail's hand slipped into Finn's. "Are you satisfied with the outcome?"

He shook his head, and for a moment, she feared the worst. Then his smile edged into view.

"Like the duke, I can only stand in awe of you. Prince Otto Leopold always strived for diplomacy rather than attack. You found a way to stop your tormenters without raising a hand."

"And only raising my voice once," she agreed with a smile. "Yet I would do it again, if it meant keeping you safe, Finn. I adore you. But this business with my father…"

"Stop," he said, suiting word to action. He took her other hand and brought both up against his chest. "Abigail Winchester, from the beginning I admired you. You are stronger than the mountains that surround my country, more beautiful than the sunrise above them. Your kindness warms me more than any fire on a winter's night while the snow flies. Yet I wondered whether I could ever have anything that I might offer the clever governess who beguiled me. Now I know. I have something that will keep others from seeking you out because of your father ever again. A name. Will you allow me to make you Abigail Huber?"

"Yes! Oh, yes!" She threw herself into his arms, rather pleased she remained composed enough to hear him out after all.

Finn held his bride-to-be close, thanksgiving filling him. He did not know what the future might bring, but with her beside him, he would be home at last.

Roth and Keller rode on the roof on the way back, but Tanner sat inside, a twinkle in his hazel eyes.

"Someone must see to Miss Winchester's reputation," he said when Finn attempted to order him out. "You have monopolized her quite enough, Huber."

"And he will continue to monopolize me," Abigail said. "I have agreed to marry him, Mr. Tanner."

Tanner's grin was the broadest Finn had seen. He turned his gaze to the window and kept it there. Once, he might have been watching for danger. Now, he gave them what privacy he could.

Lady Belfort's smile was nearly as wide when Abigail told her the news. She insisted that they explain all. Finn let Abigail do the honors. He sat beside her, gazing at the spot along the wall where he had stood so many times. Never again. His place was at her side.

Fortune must have agreed, for she had deposited herself on his lap, purring.

"Nicely done," Lady Belfort said when Abigail finished. "And now a wedding as well."

"A wedding, and a future to plan," Abigail said with a look his way.

"There, I may be of assistance." She picked up a letter from the pile on her desk. "Lord Kendall responded to my note at last. He has a village at the edge of his estate, and his steward is finding it difficult to give the place sufficient attention. He would like to engage Finn to manage it for him as a bailiff—settling disagreements, collecting rents, and recommending to his lordship what should be done to keep the villagers safe and secure. The position comes with a cottage as well as a salary."

Fortune glanced up at him, as if eager for his answer.

Finn's chest swelled. "I would be honored to take such a position. Lady Belfort, I can never thank you enough."

She held up a hand. "Thank me by giving Lord Kendall the same exemplary service you've shown here. And Abigail, I have not forgotten about you. Lady Kendall sent a note as well, asking me if I knew anyone who would be willing to take up the cause of the village school she sponsors. The children have been without a teacher for some months. They will be a handful, but with your composure and good sense, I'm sure you can bring them around."

Abigail beamed at him a moment before turning to the lady. "I would be delighted, Meredith. Thank you so much!"

Mr. Cowls came in then, though Finn suspected he had been listening near the door. "I would bring refreshments to celebrate, your ladyship, but Miss Hewett and her father are here to see you."

"Mr. Hewett instead of Miss Daring?" Lady Belfort shook her head. "Send them in, Mr. Cowls. Abigail, stay to tell them your good news and then make your escape while you can."

Of course Julia was delighted for her, squeezing Abigail's hands and going so far as to hug Finn. Her father, who had a booming voice, congratulated them as well, but she could see why Meredith had encouraged her to leave them to their discussions. His hair might be a lighter shade of red than Julia's, but his personality was even more outgoing. She had a feeling he swept everyone before him like a rushing river.

She and Finn made their excuses and left the library, Fortune surrendering him at last for the window. His hand reached for hers as they strolled down the paneled corridor.

"New positions, a new village," he mused.

"A new life," she agreed. She pulled him up short. "Oh, Finn, it is more than I ever dreamed."

"I have had dreams most of my life," he said. "Of farming in the mountains with my family, of returning to my home with my king. None of those dreams came true, but I find I cannot care. They led me here, to you."

She stepped into the circle of his arms. "Then let us plan our future, together. There is nowhere I would rather be than with my beloved bodyguard, the man who holds my heart."

Meredith cast a glance at Fortune, who was perched on the windowsill, tail swinging lazily, as she watched the drive that led toward the cottage. Another match to her credit. Small wonder she looked so pleased with herself.

Julia's father did not look nearly as pleased with his day. He and Julian had had business dealings at one time or another, and she had entertained him before. She knew him to be a force of nature, from his bristling mustache to his broad chest, and he was never shy about stating his opinions, far less charmingly than his daughter.

"The world," he announced after Abigail and Finn had left them, "has gone mad."

"Indeed," Meredith said, gaze coming back to him. "And why would you say that, sir?"

Julia sank farther in the chair. Her smile when she'd greeted Meredith had held half of its usual brightness. Her joy for Abigail and Finn had lifted her head for a time, but now she seemed to want nothing better than to make her green tailored gown melt into the leather of her seat.

"Banks are closing," her father said. "Businesses foundering. None of mine, mind you. But success can make a man a target."

Ah, so that was his purpose. She should have known he would never have called on her without Julian present if business had not been involved.

"Well," she said, sitting straighter, "then perhaps I might interest you in a bodyguard."

He slapped his hands down on the arms of his chair. "The very reason I came to see you today. Didn't I tell you Lady Belfort would be accommodating, Julia?"

"Yes," Julia said, smile strained. "Your exact word for her. Accommodating." Her look to Meredith was apologetic.

"I'm a man who looks for connections, Lady Belfort," her father said. "Perhaps this business has a printing press, and I need a catalog. Perhaps that business wants to grow, and I have money to invest. You have four strapping lads, used to playing bodyguard. I need a bodyguard."

"As you heard," Meredith said, thinking quickly, "Mr. Huber is engaged and about to join Lord Kendall's staff. Mr. Roth also has a position. He is the most experienced guard, so he may be interested in your position instead. Tell me more about what you hope. Surely here in Surrey your life isn't in any real danger."

"Everyone's life is in danger," he insisted. "Their life or their money. Cozeners like this Colonel MacGregor looking to steal your last pence. Highwaymen preying on unsuspecting travelers. Why, we heard coming through Weyton that your companion was accosted in the churchyard this very day!"

"Abigail was clearly fine, Father," Julia put in.

"Quite fine," Meredith promised her. "And in part because she had the Imperial Guards to help."

Julia's head fell to her chest, as if she'd given up all hope.

"There, you see?" her father declared before turning his bright blue eyes on Meredith. "So, which of your gentlemen would you recommend, then?"

Meredith steepled her fingers. With Julia's father so bombastic, he would likely not show the boyish Keller due respect. On the other hand, Roth would have little patience for him.

Fortune jumped from the window and came to gaze up at Meredith. Was there an answer in those copper-colored eyes?

A moment later, Tanner's voice echoed in the entry hall. Julia straightened and smoothed down her skirts.

"To be clear," her father said. "I can take care of myself. I want a man who can protect my Julia." He cleared his throat with a loud rattle. "She's all I have, you know. I could be richer than Midas, and it would mean nothing if anything should happen to her."

Julia's face melted. "Oh, Father."

Meredith smiled. "I believe I know just the fellow. He is a bit of an adventurer, but in these trying times, that's exactly the sort of man a lady needs at her side. Why don't I invite him in, and you can see for yourself."

•┼━━•⚬♥⚬•━━┼•

Thank you for choosing Abigail and Finn's story. While they are my own creation, the tragic tale of Poyais is very much a historical fact. Colonel MacGregor's lies about a golden kingdom across the seas blinded many to the truth. Banks extended him a ridiculous amount of money against his stories of riches ready for the plucking, and the Court of St. James's even recognized him. His scheme led to the deaths of dozens of hopeful settlers and contributed to an economic depression in England.

If you are curious about Prince Otto Leopold and the lives of the Imperial Guards before this story, look for *Never Pursue a Prince*. And you can read about how the Duchess and Duke of Wey came together in *Never Doubt a Duke*, only 99 cents.

But adventures lie ahead for the remaining Imperial Guards. Turn the page for a sneak peek of Julia and Tanner's story, *Never Admire an Adventurer*.

SNEAK PEEK:

BOOK TWO
GUARDING HER HEART

Never Admire an Adventurer

REGINA SCOTT

Chapter One

Near Weyton, Surrey, England
October 1825

How surprising that rebellion could feel so satisfying.

Julia Hewett had been fighting with her temper as long as she could remember. Her mother had liked to tease that a fiery red head meant a fiery heart. Generally, she did her best to get along. But her father had gone too far this time.

She settled herself on the saddle, gaze sweeping the road. Dew sparkled on the lawns that ran down from the house, making the grass look as if it were made of emeralds in the cool autumn air. A raven headed for the row of trees in the distance, black against the grey of the sky.

Any moment, her bodyguard would come riding in. Father had said it would be today, and Father was rarely wrong. That was one of the reasons he'd managed to amass a fortune great enough to buy this country estate two hours west of London. His supreme self-reliance was also why he didn't entirely trust anyone else's opinions.

Even hers.

Edevane pawed the ground, head bobbing. The feisty stallion had better things to do with his time than wait upon her good pleasure.

Julia patted the sleek black neck. "Just a few more

Never Admire an Adventurer

moments, my sweet. I'll be in a great deal of trouble if Father speaks to Mr. Tanner before I do."

She still couldn't quite believe her father had hired Kristof Tanner to act as her bodyguard. For one thing, he was a former member of the Batavarian Imperial Guard, used to protecting kings and princes, not daughters of self-made men. And for another, she hadn't seen anything approaching danger in all her three and twenty years. Her father's wealth and attention had seen to that. Yes, there had been reports of highwaymen in the area lately. And yes, her friend Abigail Winchester had nearly been kidnapped in the churchyard only last week, but that had had to do with secrets from her past.

Julia only had one secret. And he had just appeared on the horizon.

She wasn't sure how she knew it was him at that distance. The road was well traveled. Since she and Edevane had been waiting, she'd seen three carriages and four men on horseback pass. But none carried themselves with that easy confidence, as if daring the world to offer a rebuke.

Something fluttered inside her, like a moth seeking a flame. Very likely it came from the knowledge of what she must say to him.

He turned onto the drive to Hewett House and reined in beside her. "Miss Hewett. You didn't need to ride out to welcome me." His gaze traveled the gravel drive to the house. "And with no one to accompany you."

She had no intention of allowing her companion, Mrs. Daring, much less one of the grooms to hear this conversation. "I am well within sight of the house, sir," she said. "And these are my father's lands. No one would harm me here."

"Very good news," he said with a nod. "My job should be easy, then."

"Very easy," she assured him, sizing up the gelding he rode. It wouldn't be his. He must have borrowed it from Rose Hill, where he and his comrades were staying while their patroness, Lady Belfort, sought to find them positions in England now that their sovereign had returned home. "However, we must develop our strategy before you take up your position."

He cocked his head. "Strategy? I've been acting as bodyguard to King Frederick, the crown prince, and his courtiers for ten years. Do you think I need schooling?"

Heat was building in her cheeks. She ignored it. "No, of course not, though I don't doubt my father will have something to say about your responsibilities. I merely wanted to explain a few of my expectations."

He nodded toward the road. "Perhaps we can talk while we ride."

She turned Edevane, who settled in beside the gelding with a shake of his dark head. "Thank you. I understand it will be your duty to protect me whenever we leave the estate."

"Whenever you leave the house," he corrected her. "And when company calls as well."

Her father had been stricter than she'd thought. "I pity you. My life isn't that interesting."

He flashed her a smile. "Oh, I'm sure we can contrive."

Gooseflesh skittered along her arms under her wool riding habit. This, more than anything, was why she'd known she must speak to him. Kristof Tanner was a potent force on the best of days. She must not allow that attraction to pull her off her game.

"Exactly," she said. "Father will likely speak to you, if he hasn't already, about which gentlemen I'm allowed to partner at dances and such. I may at times suggest a different choice."

His mouth quirked. "Ah. You have a suitor you favor."

"Yes," she said, pleased that he'd caught on so quickly. "Viscount Westerbrook. But I haven't told Father yet. He isn't too keen on him."

Tanner urged his horse up a slight rise in the drive. Edevane took the change in elevation easily. "Not rich enough?"

"Not titled enough," Julia explained with a grimace. "Father wants a duke. I want a man who will love and honor me all the days of his life. A man I can love and honor in return. The other details don't matter one whit."

Once more his mouth quirked, as if her declaration amused him, but she could not find it in her to take offense. She probably sounded impossibly idealistic prosing on about love and honor when a good number of marriages had neither, according to her father. He saw marriage as a bargain, something else he could negotiate, as he'd negotiated his way from pit boy in a coal mine to the owner of multiple enterprises. Given such a heritage and example, surely she could negotiate a better marriage for herself.

"Very well," he said as the house loomed closer. "I'm sure we can reach an agreement."

Already she could see grooms coming out of the stable block to see to her horse and his. Any moment, a footman would open the front door as well. She felt Edevane resist as she slowed his steps.

"More importantly," she said, drawing on every ounce of courage she possessed, "we must come up with a plan about what to tell my father of our previous meetings, before we find ourselves engaged."

He had forgotten how pretty she was, how earnest. Under her short-crowned riding hat, her thick red hair was tamed back from a face with delicate features. Those big brown eyes fixed on him as if her life depended on his answer. Very likely that intensity was what had drawn him to her in the first place. That and the fact that he could never stand to see a woman cry. He had been trained to be a hero, and heroes did not stand by when needed. He could imagine that any number of men, including this Viscount Westerbrook, would be only too delighted to find themselves forced into an engagement.

But not him. He had plans for his future, and a wife could be an impediment.

So could this job. Bodyguard to an heiress. A shame it wasn't to her father. John Hewett, his patroness Lady Belfort had told him, traveled to more interesting places than shopping or the local assembly. Still, if Tanner did a good job, her father might be willing to recommend him to others who could give him the life of adventure he craved. Though not if he thought Tanner had used his daughter badly.

"I take it you haven't told him, then," he said, slowing the gelding's paces as well. Lady Belfort had allowed him the use of the horse, saying that Julia could return him when next she came to visit. If Mr. Hewett's other horses were anything like the Thoroughbred next to him, he wouldn't mind sending this horse back in exchange.

"No," she admitted. "Please understand I will be forever in your debt. I was distraught that night you discovered me in the duke's garden. You sat, you listened, you showed compassion. It was exactly what I needed."

She made him sound a paragon. He shifted on the saddle. "It was only the duty of a gentleman to a lady in distress."

"Regardless," she said, "if my father knew you and I had met alone in a moonlit garden last summer, I doubt he would have hired you to be my bodyguard. As it is, I can only be glad he was in the card room when you and I encountered each other again at the last assembly."

He was just as glad. He had no excuse for seeking her out the second time except that it had pleased him to dance with the prettiest girl in attendance at the local assembly.

He hardly wanted her father to come calling, pistol in hand. That wouldn't help either of their reputations.

"I'll say nothing," he promised. "It will be our secret."

"Thank you." She breathed out the words moments before they arrived in the stable yard.

Tanner glanced around as he dismounted. Hewett House was well situated, with fields in all directions. They would certainly see any enemy coming. The stables had multiple stalls, mostly filled, and room for three carriages, one a pony cart the lady beside him likely drove. He would need that Thoroughbred to keep up with her.

He dismounted and handed the reins to a stable boy, then turned to find one of the others had already handed her down. He wasn't sure why that disappointed him. Likely just anticipating his job as her bodyguard.

He lifted down his satchel, then fell into step beside her as she headed toward the house. It was square and solid, built of the buttery stone he was coming to equate with England. Urns at tall as a man stood on either side of the entry stairs. Good cover, if he needed it.

A tall, silver-maned fellow in a black tailcoat opened the front door for them and let them into a marble-tiled entry hall with rosewood stairs curving up one side to the next story. "Miss Hewett." He raised an impeccable brow at the sight of Tanner beside her.

"Mr. Garrison," she said, "this is Mr. Tanner, the bodyguard Father hired for me. I believe you were expecting him."

The butler's nostrils flared, as if he'd smelled something unpleasant. Tanner returned the look from a good two inches higher. Garrison raised his chin as if to make up the difference.

"Indeed," he said. "This way."

Julia sent him a commiserating look before starting up the stairs. The butler, however, led him down a corridor toward the back of the house.

Tanner quickly saw why. "The servants' stair?"

Garrison regarded him again. "Family and guests take the main stair. You are not family, and you are not a guest."

And that was where he stood in this household.

He had to turn sideways to keep his shoulders from brushing the walls as he followed the butler up the dimly lit stairs. They passed the first landing, and the second, until he wondered how there could any more floors above them. At last, Garrison came out into a corridor with multiple doors, closely spaced, opening off it. He nodded to the closest door along the right.

Tanner took two steps inside. The room didn't allow for much more than that. It had blue walls, as if he had climbed high enough to reach the sky. He could tell at a glance that the bed wasn't long enough for him to stretch out. Besides its iron frame, the room boasted a scratched bureau and washstand with a chipped pitcher. He wouldn't even have his own fire. The space was warm at the moment, but it likely would be freezing by morning. All in all, it was a far cry from the palaces in which he'd stayed for the last ten years.

"This won't do," he said, turning to the butler, who raised his brows again. "I need to be closer to Miss Hewett if I'm to protect her."

"If your protection is required," Garrison said, doubt lacing every syllable, "you will be called for."

"If you wait until the danger is here, calling for me may be too late," Tanner pointed out. "And where do you intend for me to store my short sword, knives, pistols, and ammunition? They'll be coming by carriage tomorrow."

Garrison drew himself up. "I am quite certain you won't need any of that here."

"Perhaps we should speak with Mr. Hewett," Tanner tried. "There seems to be a misunderstanding as to my role."

The butler affixed him with a steely eye, reminding

him a little of Stephen Roth, the oldest of his friends to remain in England. "Mr. Hewett has already conveyed his wishes to me on the matter. You will find, Mr. Tanner, that he has a particular way of doing things and does not like his routine disturbed. And neither do I."

Tanner thumped his fist against his chest. The butler frowned.

"Sorry," Tanner said. "That is how we recognize our superiors in Batavaria."

His mouth twitched, but he did not go so far as to smile. "Very wise. You will be sent for when you are needed."

He glided out of the room so smoothly that Tanner tipped his head to make sure the fellow wasn't on wheels. Then he straightened and dropped his satchel on the bed. It didn't bounce.

"Welcome, indeed," he muttered.

Very likely he was expected to sit on that hard bed as he waited. He had grown used to waiting along the wall as his sovereign attended state functions. But the King of Batavaria had never hidden him away in a cupboard. Neither had Lady Belfort.

So, he used the cold water in the pitcher to rub the travel dirt from his face and hands. No time to shave, though only a little scruff was growing after this morning. Besides, he was a bodyguard, not the lady's suitor.

You could be.

He shook the odd thought away. If he wanted Mr. Hewett to see him as worthy of his trust and recommendation, he would have to be very, very careful not to show how much he already admired his charming daughter. He was a bodyguard. That was all.

But he couldn't do his job with no line of sight, no chance of hearing. Surely Mr. Hewett would understand that.

He thought about using the main stairs, but decided not to flaunt the house rules any more than necessary.

Squeezing his way down the servants' stairs, he checked each floor for the layout and security. The floor immediately below his was all bedchambers, spaced much farther apart and far better appointed. The floor below that held a library, dining room, and withdrawing room. The raised voices coming from the last urged him forward.

Now, this was a room worthy of a palace. Every wall was covered in flocked emerald wallpaper from the floor to the high ceiling, which was inlaid with gilded flowers linked by plaster branches. The massive landscape painting over the white marble hearth was framed in gold. The carpet was thick enough to silence any footfall.

Though boots echoing on hardwood would not have been heard against the argument.

"It's an important decision, marriage," Mr. Hewett was saying from his spot near a window that overlooked the grounds. "Too important to be left to chance."

Julia, standing by the hearth and now dressed in a pretty green frock, narrowed her eyes at him. "And you think my intelligence and education have in no way equipped me to make a choice that has nothing to do with chance?"

Now her father's eyes narrowed, a far more intimidating look. Her eyes were a warm brown. His were a cool blue. Even his red hair was a lighter shade than hers.

"What do you mean," he said slowly, "education?"

Tanner bristled at the tone and scolded himself.

Julia snorted. "My tutelage by various governesses, dancing masters, language instructors, musicians, and painters."

Her father relaxed. "Oh, that. Well, they may have taught you all the arts required of a lady, but I doubt they taught you how to find the right lord."

He was determined to thwart her. By the way her head came up, Julia intended to match him.

But another movement caught his eye. The white-haired woman who served as Julia's chaperone was tiny enough she nearly blended into the sofa. She had an improbable name of Mrs. Daring, if he recalled. At the moment, she looked as if she wanted nothing more than to escape the escalating conflict.

"I already found the perfect lord," Julia told her. "Someone dashing and considerate and intelligent, who thinks I walk on water."

So, she was going to tell him about Westerbrook. He could only hope her gambit paid off.

Her father chuckled. "Well, that's a start at least. Duke, marquess, earl?"

"An Englishman whose family goes back before the Conquest," she assured him.

He leaned against the windowsill. "The name, my girl."

"Viscount Westerbrook."

Red flamed into her father's cheeks, until they clashed with his hair. "No."

She clenched her fists, and Tanner wouldn't have been surprised if she counted to ten before answering him.

"Yes. He is my choice. The sooner you accept that, the better for us both."

"No," her father repeated, crossing his arms over his chest. "He's a weak-willed spendthrift with no ambition."

"He knows his own mind," she insisted, taking a step forward. "If he spends money, it's because he has money and the exquisite taste to use it well. And he doesn't need ambition. He's reached the pinnacle of achievement."

"Ha! That's just a fancy way of saying he's too lazy to move forward."

Now her fists reached her waist. "You didn't complain when he invested in your railroad."

"I don't mind taking money from fools," he said complacently. "I just don't want them marrying my daughter." He pushed off from the sill. "Think, Julia. I've arranged to put the world at your feet. Don't throw it away on a good-for-nothing with a pretty face and a fast horse."

"Very well," she said, and the hair rose on the back of Tanner's neck. He had heard danger coming many a time. This was it.

"Then I'll marry Mr. Tanner instead," she declared. "After all, he's already compromised me."

Learn more at
www.reginascott.com/adventurer.html

OTHER BOOKS BY REGINA SCOTT

Fortune's Brides Series
Never Doubt a Duke
Never Borrow a Baronet
Never Envy an Earl
Never Vie for a Viscount
Never Kneel to a Knight
Never Marry a Marquess
Always Kiss at Christmas
Never Pursue a Prince
Never Court a Count
Never Romance a Rogue
Never Love a Lord
Never Beguile a Bodyguard

Grace-by-the-Sea Series
The Matchmaker's Rogue
The Heiress's Convenient Husband
The Artist's Healer
The Governess's Earl
The Lady's Second-Chance Suitor
The Siren's Captain

Uncommon Courtships Series
The Unflappable Miss Fairchild
The Incomparable Miss Compton
The Irredeemable Miss Renfield
The Unwilling Miss Watkin
An Uncommon Christmas

Lady Emily Capers
Secrets and Sensibilities
Art and Artifice
Ballrooms and Blackmail
Eloquence and Espionage
Love and Larceny

Marvelous Munroes Series
My True Love Gave to Me
The Rogue Next Door
The Marquis' Kiss
A Match for Mother

Spy Matchmaker Series
The Husband Mission
The June Bride Conspiracy
The Heiress Objective

The Regent's Devices Trilogy
(writing as R.E. Scott with Shelley Adina)
The Emperor's Aeronaut
The Prince's Pilot
The Lady's Triumph

Frontier Matches
The Perfect Mail-Order Bride
Her Frontier Sweethearts

And other books from Harper Collins, Mirror Press, and Revell.

About the Author

Regina Scott started writing novels in the third grade. Thankfully for literature as we know it, she didn't sell her first novel until she learned a bit more about writing. Since her first book was published, her stories have traveled the globe, with translations in many languages including Dutch, German, Italian, and Portuguese. She now has more than 60 published works of warm, witty romance, and more than one million copies of her books are in reader hands.

Alas, she cannot have a cat of her own, as her husband is allergic to them. Fortune the cat belongs to her critique partner and dear friend Kristy J. Manhattan, who supports pet rescue groups and spoils her four-footed family members. If Fortune resembles any cat you know, credit Kristy.

Regina Scott and her husband of 30 years reside in the Puget Sound area of Washington State. She has dressed as a Regency dandy, driven four-in-hand, learned to fence, and sailed on a tall ship, all in the name of research, of course. Learn more about her at www.reginascott.com.